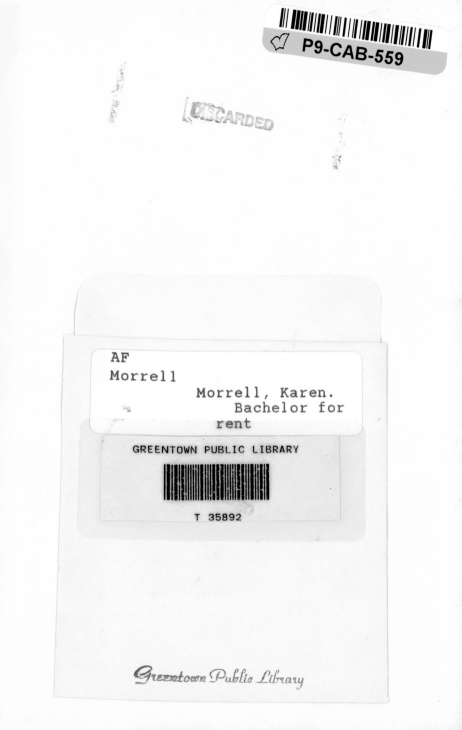

BACHELOR FOR RENT

BACHELOR FOR RENT

•

KAREN MORRELL

AVALON BOOKS
THOMAS BOUREGY AND COMPANY, INC.
401 LAFAYETTE STREET
NEW YORK, NEW YORK 10003

© Copyright 1993 by Karen Morrell
Library of Congress Catalog Card Number: 93-90591
ISBN 0-8034-9011-9

PRINTED IN THE UNITED STATES OF AMERICA
ON ACID-FREE PAPER
BY HADDON CRAFTSMEN, SCRANTON, PENNSYLVANIA

This book is dedicated to two very special groups of friends.

My Michigan critique group: Linda Bartell, Linda Pedder, Lucy Taylor, Kathy Tountas, and Joyce Wells.

And, my Texas critique group: Dora Brown, Judy Christenberry, Anne Franklin, Barbara Harrison, Pat Hein, Stephanie Howell, Karen Leabo, and Marty Masters.

Without you, my dreams would still be dreams.

Chapter 1

"**N**o."

"What do you mean, 'no'?"

Sarah Perkins took a deep breath and exhaled slowly and deliberately, all the while keeping her slate gray eyes riveted on the impeccably dressed woman seated across the table from her.

"What I mean, Mother, is there's absolutely no way I can drop everything and run off to the Caribbean."

Andora Lavelle took a long sip of her spiced tea, then smiled at her only daughter. "You look tired, Sarah. You need to get away, to take a vacation."

"Needing one and taking one are two different things."

Sarah's response brought forth a softly snorted reply from her mother.

"I can't abandon Brad on such short notice. We're still swamped with paperwork from the sale of that high-rise condominium."

Andora waved away her daughter's protests with a slim, red-nailed hand. "Bradley Ferguson can do without your services for three days. You spend entirely

1

too much time in that stuffy little real estate office anyway. Besides, I've already made all the arrangements for your trip, and it's too late to cancel.''

From experience, Sarah knew that trying to convince her mother through logical reasoning was a lost cause. Andora was used to getting her own way, and once she made up her mind, no one could persuade her to change it.

A waiter quietly placed a basket of warm cinnamon rolls on their table and poured more tea. Andora nodded her gratitude.

''What about the Harrison estate?'' Sarah continued after the man had left. ''I've been working with Roger and Pauline Harrison for three months. I finally found a suitable buyer and I can't abandon them now. The closing is scheduled for Saturday morning, and I know there'll be complications. Who'll take care of it if I'm sunning myself on a beach somewhere?'' Although her partner was highly competent, Sarah prided herself on seeing projects through to completion. Especially projects that involved elderly, easily confused clients like the Harrisons.

''Try to reschedule it, dear. Make a few phone calls. It won't be as difficult as you think.'' Andora nibbled on a sweet roll then daintily dusted the corners of her mouth with a linen napkin. ''You owe it to yourself, Sarah. For once in your life, live a little. Escape!''

''That kind of life-style suits *you*,'' Sarah reminded her mother. ''You're going to a fund raiser rally this afternoon, and if my memory is correct you're hosting a meet-the-candidate party tonight, and in a couple of weeks you'll take off for Paris.''

Andora nodded and took another sip of tea. ''If you recall, I offered to take you with me.''

''Mother, you know I can't afford to take off—''

''Nonsense!'' Andora protested. ''I invited you as my guest. It wouldn't have cost you a dime.''

Sarah sighed and shook her head. ''It's not an issue of money. I can't afford to take time away from the office. I have fifteen listings—''

Andora threw her arms into the air. ''Listen to yourself! You spend more time at work than two normal people. You turn on the lights every morning and close up shop every night. Your social life is nonexistent. You've become one of those dreadful workaholics.''

''Mother, please—'' Sarah began, but Andora rushed on.

''Working eighteen hours a day and hiding your head in a stack of paperwork isn't going to bring David back. He's gone, Sarah. Do you honestly believe he'd have wanted you to isolate yourself from life itself?''

Sarah silently shook her head, her mother's words bringing a familiar jab of pain to her heart. An image of David's laughing blue eyes and irresistible grin floated through her mind. Would she always have this feeling of loss when she thought of David?

They had been so perfectly suited, so happy together. Then a week after they'd announced their engagement,

David had been killed. A senseless, tragic, random killing.

While Sarah would never admit as much to anyone, she knew her mother was right. The reason Sarah drove herself so relentlessly in her work was to keep too busy to think about him.

"Whatever happened to Timothy what's-his-name?" Andora prompted.

Sarah shrugged. She couldn't remember his last name either. "Timothy simply treated me to dinner after I helped him sell his duplex. He's a nice man who—"

"Who, if you had encouraged him, would be adding some spice to your life," Andora interjected.

Sarah groaned inwardly. She didn't question her mother's conclusion. Andora had more experience when it came to men, far more. "Timothy wasn't my type," Sarah said flatly, then glanced at her watch. She had to go. A busy afternoon loomed ahead of her. She had to investigate the probability of two clients securing bank loans, review an appraisal, and write and post a newspaper advertisement. The list went on and on.

She scooted to the edge of her chair. "Thanks for my birthday lunch, Mother."

" 'And for the trip to St. Maarten, Mother,' " Andora added.

Sarah massaged her aching temples. The thought of escaping from the confines of a frigid Michigan January to lounge at a tropical resort was more than a little appealing. She was also confident that Bradley, once her boss and recently her business partner, could manage without her for a few days.

What harm could there be in finally taking advantage of one of her mother's tempting offers, which she had been refusing for the past several years? She could tell by the triumphant look gleaming in her mother's eyes that the older woman knew the instant her daughter had acquiesced.

"Then it's settled," Andora said smugly. With a feminine flick of her tiny wrist, she summoned the waiter to bring their check. Then, reaching into the black leather suitcase she called a "purse," she produced an envelope of travel documents. Andora slid the papers across the starched white linen tablecloth to within Sarah's reach. Then she clasped her hands in her lap and smiled her beguiling chairwoman's smile, which she employed frequently with committee members. "The plane leaves tomorrow at eleven-thirty. I'll send someone for you around ten."

The maitre d' arrived to assist Andora from her seat just as she eased her chair from the table. "Thank you, Henry," she purred, fluttering her eyelashes appropriately. Then turning her attention back to Sarah, she added, "And, darling, pack some of those sensational ensembles you've been hoarding. Why you insist on dressing so conservatively is beyond me." She shook her head, reached for Henry's proffered arm, and blew

Sarah a kiss. "Happy birthday, honey. Call me when you get back."

Sarah felt a mixture of irritation and amusement as she watched her mother exit the restaurant. Stopping to exchange hellos with several other diners, Andora never released her firm grip from the gracious host's elbow. Her glossy, wavy hair had been tinted to an ageless blonde. The skillful application of her makeup accentuated her high cheekbones and deeply set eyes, while the lines of her platinum wool skirt and matching jacket effectively displayed her stunning figure.

As Sarah left the table unassisted, she scrutinized her own wool suit. The three-piece outfit was typical of her own style. Dusty-rose in color, it was a simple design with no excess trimmings. She had no desire to gain the kind of attention from men that her mother received. What had it ever gotten Andora besides broken promises from dashing losers and one failed marriage after another?

Andora, like Sarah, had experienced a once-in-a-lifetime, fairy-tale romance in her early twenties. After Sarah's father was killed in a boating accident, Andora had remarried three times, and was also thrice divorced. True love could never be replaced. Sarah believed that from the bottom of her heart.

She had absolutely no intention of making the same mistakes her mother had made. She would never follow in the wake of her mother's disasters.

*   *   *

Sarah slammed the lid of her suitcase and locked it. She sank onto a soft chintz chair and stared grimly at the two pieces of burgundy-colored luggage, tennis racket, and canvas tote bag that waited at the foot of her bed, ominously reminding her of her mother's maneuverings in the past.

A mere twenty-one hours ago she hadn't had the faintest idea she'd be packing for a three-day trip to St. Maarten. She grimaced. This wasn't the first time her mother had thrown Sarah's entire life into disarray.

A solid rapping sound brought Sarah to her feet. She lugged the travel paraphernalia down the stairs and dropped it in a heap on the polished hardwood floor of the foyer. When she opened the door, her breath caught in her throat.

Instead of Charles, her mother's trusty chauffeur, a fair-haired stranger filled Sarah's doorway.

A gust of Arctic air tore the storm door from her fingers and sent her shoulder-length chestnut hair blowing in all directions.

"Richard Collier at your service, ma'am," the man said, managing to capture the errant door.

"Please come in while I get my coat," Sarah finally managed to say, still wondering what had happened to Charles.

Without a moment's hesitation the blond stranger stepped into the house and extended his hand. "It's a pleasure to meet you, Sarah."

His fingers were warm and strong as they touched

hers. She felt a tingle of expectancy flow through her and quickly released his palm. Sarah's gaze traveled up the camel-colored coat, up over the wide shoulders, past the squared jaw and thick, bushy mustache, beyond the nose with a sprinkling of light freckles to the bluest pair of eyes she'd ever seen.

She swallowed and moistened her suddenly parched lips with the tip of her tongue. "I'll get my coat," she repeated, silently chiding herself for being so taken by the man. When she reached for the closet door, a large hand grasped the knob before her fingers could make contact.

"Allow me." Richard flashed her a smile that would do a dentist proud.

This one's a real charmer, she thought, reaching into the dark cubicle and removing her London Fog rain coat. He immediately took the garment from her and held it as she eased her arms into the sleeves.

"Are you sure you'll be warm enough in this?" he asked.

Sarah gave him a curious look. "I like to travel light," she ventured, continuing to ponder when and why her mother had made a new addition to her staff. After wrapping a silk scarf around her hair and artfully forming a soft bow under her chin, she bent to retrieve her purse from the floor.

She watched in fascination as the sizable gentleman lifted her luggage as if it were filled with feathers instead of her survival gear for the weekend. Balancing it entirely in his right hand and arm, he opened the front door and made a sweeping motion to indicate Sarah should proceed to the car.

A shiny silver BMW was parked at the end of the path of stepping stones that led to her driveway. Charles normally drove her mother's white Lincoln, Sarah noted, wondering if Andora had traded in cars as well as drivers.

Richard opened the passenger door for her, then carried her luggage around to the driver's side and slid it onto the backseat. It was strange that he didn't use the trunk, Sarah thought, watching as he inserted the key into the ignition. A sonorous rhapsody pealed from the tape player filling the interior of the car with music. Richard adjusted the volume before he pulled onto the street.

"Sorry about that. I like to get the full effect of the orchestra," he explained. "If you prefer, I can turn it off."

"Actually, I'm very fond of Mantovani." And, she added silently, she was also relieved that small talk won't be necessary.

"Will this be your first trip to St. Maarten?" Richard asked a few minutes later, as he accelerated from the entrance ramp onto the congested freeway.

This was idle conversation, she decided. Long ago she'd learned how to give short, succinct responses that hinted at her dislike of trivial chit-chat. "Yes,"

Sarah answered simply. She stared at her hands folded primly in her lap.

"Do you golf?"

"Barely." She stifled a smile, remembering the last time she had played with Bradley's wife. After catching Richard's questioning glance, she continued. "I chase my ball around the course and get lots of advice from the poor person paired up with me."

When he laughed, she furrowed her brow and scrutinized his profile. Who *was* this man? Sarah hesitated to bluntly ask if he was a chauffeur in case he was just doing her mother or Charles a favor by driving her. How could she delicately find out who he was?

"Are you a friend of my mother's?" she ventured after several minutes of deliberation.

Again he chuckled. "I think half the state of Michigan claims to be a friend of Andora's."

Sarah could certainly agree with that observation. Especially the population of men between eighteen and eighty.

Richard glanced in the rearview mirror, then he pulled onto the lane marked Detroit Metropolitan Airport. "Would you like me to drop you off at the gate?" he asked, maneuvering the BMW through the traffic.

"Please," Sarah answered, then wondered why he would ask such an unnecessary question.

He pulled up to the curb reserved for Coastal Airlines departures and parked. A blast of wind blew down the collar of his coat as he hefted her leather bags and tennis racket from the car.

Without a backward glance, she stepped from the car, then reached into the side pocket of her purse and produced her ticket. She gave it to the redcap who had already loaded her belongings onto a cart.

"Right this way," the porter instructed as he led the way to the curbside check-in station.

Sarah turned to Richard, who was still standing next to the car. "Thanks for dropping me off. I'll find my way from here." She paused momentarily and waited for him to bid her good-bye.

Instead, he raked his hands through his hair. A frown creased his brow. For a moment they merely stood on the windy sidewalk engulfed in the smell of diesel fumes from a commuter bus making its way into the sea of cars.

Finally, Sarah gave him a polite smile and walked into the terminal. His lack of farewell puzzled her. At least he might have wished her a good trip, she thought with a spark of sudden irritation.

In her typical no-nonsense manner, she walked through the concourse in quick, efficient steps, looking neither left nor right. At the end of the corridor, she glanced at the monitor and headed toward gate thirty-four. When she arrived, she discovered the other passengers were already beginning to board. She took her place in line to receive her seat assignment.

Once on the plane, she stowed her purse and coat

in the overhead compartment and slumped onto seat 3A. How like her mother to reserve first-class accommodations, Sarah thought.

When a flight attendant offered her a magazine and a complimentary cocktail, Sarah declined both. Her stomach quivered and rumbled. In an attempt to settle her nerves, she sat up a little straighter, fastened her seatbelt, and took several deep, slow breaths. Flying on a calm summer day was bad enough, but taking off into a howling winter wind would be something else. She clenched her hands together into a tight ball of white knuckles.

Glancing impatiently at her watch, she saw that it was five minutes until departure. The seat next to hers was still unoccupied, which pleased her to no end. She'd brought along the recent edition of the Multiple Listing Guide to analyze the new homes that had recently come on the market.

Sarah made it her business to keep up not only with the listings of her own agency but with those of other agencies as well. Her commission for selling their properties was not as large as selling those of her own agency, but the important thing was to fulfill the customer's needs. A satisfied client usually came back to the same agent when he or she was ready to sell or to invest in additional property. Sarah hadn't worked herself up to top agent in Middletown for residential sales by resting on her laurels.

But now was the time to relax, Sarah reminded herself. She leaned her head against the window, closed her eyes, and took a deep breath. Perhaps she should try to take a short nap. The flight would certainly pass more quickly that way. But seconds later, Sarah became instantly alert at the sound of a man's irritated voice.

"If this is your idea of a joke, I don't appreciate it."

When Sarah opened her eyes she was shocked to discover none other than Richard Collier standing in the aisle facing her. His expression was angry, his stance imposing.

Sarah blinked in confusion. "What are you doing here? Did I forget something?"

"You forgot something all right. Me."

"You?" Sarah struggled to understand, and then it hit her. "Oh, my goodness, I'm so sorry." Reaching beneath the seat in front of her, she quickly withdrew her checkbook from her purse. "I just assumed Mother had paid you. It never occurred to me—"

"Sarah, Andora took care of all the details—"

"Then why are you here?" Sarah interrupted. "If I didn't forget anything . . . "

"You forgot *me*."

Him? Sarah's dismay instantly transformed into mortification when she noticed the carry-on luggage at his side.

"I'm occupying seat 3B," Richard continued. "Didn't you think we'd be sitting together?"

Her heart gave an alarming leap. "Oh, no. Surely

you can't mean . . . '' Sarah let her words trail off as Richard Collier nodded his confirmation.

Her mother had not only paid for her plane and hotel reservations, but for an escort as well! Of all the underhanded, conniving, sneaky schemes, Sarah fumed, this one took the prize!

"I thought I was traveling alone," she said in a rigidly controlled voice.

"Obviously you're not," Richard returned, still scowling.

Color flooded Sarah's cheeks. "I think there has been a mistake. If you hurry, you probably have enough time to get off the plane."

"Is everything all right, sir?" a flight attendant asked before Richard could move an inch.

"Just perfect," he mumbled, shifting his bag to his other hand.

"Fine, then please have a seat and buckle-up for takeoff," the redheaded attendant prompted.

Sarah's eyes widened with comprehension. Richard Collier had no intention of quietly retreating back to whence he had come. Her cheeks stung with anger.

"You can't come with me," she protested, as he took off his coat. *Don't lose your temper*, she ordered herself. *Try to stay calm*. "Be reasonable, Mr. Collier. There's been an awful misunderstanding. You're going to have to get off this plane." Her voice was drowned out by the noise of the jet's powerful engines.

"Right," he murmured, giving her a brief glance.

"Would you like me to squeeze through a window and jump from the wing?"

Sarah sank back into her seat as he began his search for an empty bin to stash his coat and bag. He was opening them and banging them shut as though he had every right in the world to cause over a hundred people to wait.

If he wanted to create a scene that would broadcast his tardiness to everyone from the cockpit to the last row, that was up to him, Sarah thought. She simply planned to look the other way and have nothing to do with his little display of temper.

But when he raised his arms and firmly shoved his belongings into a corner of the already filled compartment above her, Sarah couldn't help but notice how his light blue knit shirt fit just tight enough to emphasize the solid breadth of his shoulders and the sinewy muscles in his chest. He must have played football or trained as a weight lifter to develop his body like that, she reflected with instinctive disdain. A jock. She might have known.

Richard finally took his seat and immediately stretched above his head to open the vent in an effort to increase the air flow. He folded his arms across his chest and turned toward Sarah. "Well, we're off."

"I don't believe it," she muttered angrily.

"Likewise," he grumbled, then fastened his seatbelt with an emphatic snap.

"My own mother set me up!"

"Apparently," Richard said, "she set us both up. Andora seemed to think you would enjoy my company. Obviously she was wrong."

"Obviously."

Richard shifted in his seat and ran his fingers around the collar of his shirt.

Sarah tried to ignore him.

A few seconds later as the jet climbed in altitude, she clutched her fingers around the armrests and held her breath. When she felt the reassuring thud of the landing gear slipping into its in-flight position, she released her fingers and breathed a small sigh of relief. At least they were off the ground safely.

She attempted to stretch her legs only to find that her seatmate was using not only his own floor space but hers as well. When the tips of her navy pumps came in contact with a gigantic leather boot, she quickly recoiled her legs against the seat.

She chided herself for being in this predicament in the first place. She should have known never, ever to accept one of her mother's gifts at face value. More often than not, there was a little catch. She glanced at Richard Collier. This time her mother had outdone herself! A man. Her mother had bought her a man!

What was she going to do?

Sarah pondered this disturbing question while she studied the cloud formations spreading beneath her.

Chapter 2

Richard reached for the complimentary magazine shoved into the protruding pouch that poked his knees. Given time to analyze the situation and with his insight into Andora Lavelle's personality, he had been able to surmise fairly quickly that Sarah knew nothing about the travel arrangements.

No wonder she'd left him standing in the bus fumes on the curb, he thought, flipping through the tattered pages of the magazine. He ventured a glance at her. By the vexed expression on her face, he knew that this excursion would be anything but a pleasure trip. It was impossible not to feel the hostile vibrations emanating from his new acquaintance.

He remembered how her entire body trembled when the plane had taxied into position and began rolling down the runway, gathering speed for takeoff. Could she fear flying? he wondered. He'd been tempted to say something reassuring, but decided against it.

Her cold-shoulder treatment of him strengthened his initial impression of her as a reserved, unsociable woman. Although he and the flamboyant Andora had served as cochairman of the committee to fund a new wing for the Children's Hospital, he had not met her daughter. Until today.

Though the two shared the same shade of deep, pearly gray eyes, it seemed that was where the similarities ended, he thought with a disgruntled sigh.

Richard tucked the magazine between his thigh and the armrest and pressed the button to recline his seat. His thoughts drifted back to that fateful day in December when Andora had lured him into this "opportunity to have a little fun in the sun."

He was way behind in his goal to raise fifty thousand dollars in donations for new oncology equipment by the first of February. When Andora had hinted that her pledges already exceeded her goal and then offered to help him secure more than ten thousand dollars toward the fund, his interest was piqued. Seated next to her at the mayor's Christmas party in the crowded ballroom at the Foster Hotel, Richard remembered nodding his consent to include himself in her plan.

When the mayor beckoned Andora to join him at the podium a half hour later, and she announced her idea for the epitome of fund raisers, Richard wanted to crawl to the nearest exit.

Andora Lavelle had proclaimed that on the twenty-third of January, The Children's Hospital Development Committee would sponsor Middletown's first Bachelor-for-Rent extravaganza. She went on to say that none other than Richard Collier had graciously volunteered to serve as one of the eligible bachelors to stand on the auction block.

For a lingering moment Richard studied the woman seated next to him on the plane. His date could have been a lot worse, he reflected. The night of the auction Andora stepped in at the last minute and outbid the diamond-clad woman with the tinted lavender hair who wore a purple satin jumpsuit. She could've been sitting in seat 3A instead of Sarah Perkins.

She really was an attractive woman, he mused. Her dark brown hair was thick and lustrous, just barely brushing her shoulders. She wore it loose, so the tips curved under with a fringe of bangs over her forehead. The style suited her, Richard decided. It was sophisticated with an understated elegance.

When the object of his attention turned in his direction, he found himself staring into a pair of clear gray eyes.

"This is so . . . humiliating," she began.

"Why?"

"Why!" she practically shrieked, then obviously remembering where they were, continued more quietly, "because my mother . . . bought you."

Richard was momentarily at a loss for words. Then it struck him. She thought he was a hired escort. A gigolo. His first instinct was to correct her preposterous assumption pronto. However, at the same time, it both irked and amused him to realize that this was the first time he'd ever been mistaken for a womanizing playboy. On a sudden impulse, he decided to keep his identity a secret.

An avid chess player, he knew how to apply strategic moves, such as opening traps, attacks, endgames, and of course, checkmate. He prided himself on being able to carefully and concisely analyze the most critical situations—an ability that enabled even a novice to turn the tables on a more experienced player. Such knowledge would come in handy if he intended to keep a step ahead of Sarah Perkins.

"Why not just think of it as a blind date?" he countered finally. "Would that make you feel better?"

"No." Sarah's lips grew taut, her expression grim.

"You sound as if you speak from experience," he observed. Watching her intense glare at the striped fabric on the back of Seat 2A, Richard hid a smile. She was going to be absolutely livid when she found out that he'd deliberately avoided revealing the true circumstances behind their trip.

"Your mother was only trying to treat you to a good time. You certainly can't fault her for that," he told Sarah.

She snapped her head around to face him. Her eyes flashed sparks. "Oh yes I can!"

Her narrow-eyed glare prompted him to smile. "Be a good sport and relax a little."

Sarah closed her eyes. She was a good sport all right. During the course of her childhood, every time her mother had announced her intention to remarry, Sarah had been a good sport about that too. She'd hidden her heartbreak behind an nonchalant air.

Now, as Richard embarked into a friendly conversation with the young, red-haired flight attendant, Sarah tried to dismiss the masculine cadence of his voice. She only had to tolerate his presence for a little while. A man with his good looks and easy charm could take his pick of unattached women at a resort. And she felt sure he would.

Never in a million years would she have sought such a man on her own. Indeed, she thought of the man's occupation, of the many woman he must have ''escorted'' over the years. She was appalled. And embarrassed. She would certainly never pay for male companionship. But her mother had. For *her*! That revelation added to her mortification. Her stomach constricted into a tight knot of embitterment.

An hour later after trying in vain to study the listing guide, Sarah took another sip of Diet Coke and openly stared at the now sleeping man she'd been given for her birthday. ''The woman is completely without conscience,'' she whispered softly to his slumbering profile.

When the faintest of smiles curved the tips of his mustache, indicating that he was now wide awake, Sarah felt all the more embarrassed.

Propping his elbow on the armrest, he cupped his chin on his hand. ''I assume you're referring to your mother.''

"Yes, my mother," Sarah said. She folded her hands across her knees and concentrated on relaxing. "Did you know she's had four husbands?"

Sarah expected him to make some comment. When instead he only nodded, she went further than she'd intended. "She's the most incorrigible romantic I know. How she spends her own life is her business, but I refuse to let her make a mockery of mine." With that, she turned in her seat and faced the window.

Though Andora's sense of priorities seemed sadly scrambled, Richard knew she loved her daughter. And she was concerned about Sarah's emotional well-being. After all, Andora had kept insisting that a weekend of male companionship was just what her daughter needed to rejuvenate her spirits and, at least temporarily, relieve the pressures that she experienced as a new business owner.

From outward appearances, Andora was right, Richard thought. The results of Sarah's long days were obvious. She was tense and edgy. All of his instincts told him that this woman would prefer a quiet weekend alone. She'd probably avoid him at all costs. But, he was a man who rose to a challenge.

Turning his attention back to his crossword puzzle, Richard tapped his pencil against the in-flight magazine. "I don't suppose you'd know a seven-letter word for decrepit, third letter *c*, ends with *t*."

An ardent puzzle worker herself, Sarah only had to think for a minute before the solution became evident.

"Try ancient." And that's exactly how she felt, she added silently. It seemed like she'd been a grown-up all her life.

"Hey, you're right." He turned to face her. "Have you worked this one before?"

Sarah shook her head and focused her eyes on his thick, tawny-gold hair. "How old are you?" she asked.

"Thirty-two."

"That old?" She would have guessed he was no more than twenty-five.

Slowly, with the corners of his eyes crinkling in a most effective way, he smiled. "And how old are you?"

Sarah frowned. "Old, decrepit, ancient."

"Oh, come on. Andora can't be a day over forty-five. So that makes you what, about twenty-five?"

"For your information, last October my mother celebrated her fifty-sixth birthday. And today I'm celebrating my twenty-eighth." Her voice was cool and crisp.

"Well, happy birthday! Have you planned anything special?"

His teasing inquiry brought a trace of a smile to Sarah's lips. "Oh no," she said, raising her eyes to meet his. "I planned on having a regular, run-of-the-mill type day. Get up at the crack of dawn, pack a few things, fly to the Caribbean, and be entertained by a *hired escort*." His amused expression increased her irritation.

Hoping to puncture his inflated air of sophistication, Sarah blurted the first question that came to her mind. "Do your parents know what you do for a living?"

"Of course."

"And they don't mind?"

"Why should they mind?"

Sarah shrugged and wished she was up to her neck in real estate contracts instead of sitting shoulder to shoulder with someone she considered to be dangerous.

"Actually," he continued without further prompting, "my parents are quite proud of me."

"Oh?"

"Uh huh." He grinned.

By the time lunch was over and the trays had been removed, Sarah had learned a great deal about Richard's family. His younger brother had recently married and moved to Texas. His father and mother owned a pharmacy. And something must have happened during Richard's high school years that still brought a pained expression to his face and a faraway look to his eyes.

After a brief layover in San Juan, Puerto Rico, they reached their final destination of St. Maarten just before sunset. Whispering palms and the lush scent of tropical foliage awakened Sarah's lagging senses as the automatic doors slid open, and she stepped into the garden paradise that surrounded the Princess Julian Airport.

Richard hailed a taxi parked at the curb. "Silver Sands Hotel," he told the driver.

The man loaded their luggage into the trunk and then headed shoreward toward Simpson Bay.

"We'll be staying on the Dutch side of the island," Richard informed Sarah. "Most of the hotels are near Phillipsburg. We should be there in less than ten minutes."

Sarah flashed him a skeptical glance. How many other women had he escorted here? Was this his favorite spot for an all-expenses-paid romantic getaway?

Finally, her curiosity got the better of her, and she had to ask. "Have you been here before?"

"Nope." His mouth expanded into an irresistible grin, as if he were able to slip into her mind and plunge into her thoughts. "But I like to read, and it's amazing how many facts you can find in a guidebook."

At least he takes his job seriously, Sarah thought, concluding that might be his only socially redeeming attribute.

A hibiscus-covered arbor marked the entrance to their hotel. Ceiling fans stirred the balmy air. The spacious lobby smelled like a delicate mixture of florals and lemon. They walked over bamboo mats that were strewn across the parquet floor bordering the registration desk.

A young, deeply tanned female hotel employee watched them approach. Her gaze moved appreciatively up Richard's torso and over his face before her eyes met his. He took the brief, appraising look with a polite smile and waited for the woman to speak.

"Welcome to the Silver Sands." Her words dripped with sweetness. "May I help you?"

"Reservations for Collier." His voice was resonant and impressive, Sarah noted. Obviously he was a man aware of his looks and comfortable with them.

The woman flipped through her logbook and broke into a wide smile when the tip of her long, magenta-colored nail came to rest on his name. "Yes, Dr. Collier. I have your reservations right here." Her eyelashes fluttered provocatively. "Adjoining rooms, ocean view, two nights. Is that correct?"

Richard merely nodded his confirmation.

"Please sign here," she purred, slipping a hotel pen between the thumb and index finger of his right hand.

Richard immediately transferred the pen to his left hand and scrawled his signature.

Sarah peered over his shoulder and arched her brows inquiringly. *Dr.* Richard Collier? There must be some mistake. Perhaps he'd invented the title in order to guarantee first-rate service and accommodations.

"Please let me know if there's anything I can do to make your stay more enjoyable," the sultry beauty cooed.

Why don't you just leap over the counter into his arms? Sarah thought in disgust. Honestly, the way some women carried on.

"Shall we?" Richard offered his elbow to Sarah as a doddering, white-haired porter pushed their luggage cart toward the elevator. Instead of taking his arm, she clutched the straps of her purse and walked several paces behind him.

When they came to room 437, the bellhop drew a door key from his vest pocket and inserted it deftly into the lock.

"All the luggage can go in this room," Richard instructed. They watched while the man unloaded their bags, then Richard slipped a folded bill into the valet's outstretched hand. He awarded Richard a wide smile, tipped the brim of his cap, then sauntered down the corridor.

Sarah walked coolly past her escort and into the room. Richard followed, closing the door behind him. She placed her hands on her hips, took a deep breath, then turned to face him.

"I think we'd better get a few things straight, *Dr.* Collier."

Richard held up his hand to silence her. "Don't get yourself in a huff, Sarah. I didn't want to send that old guy into a coronary from lifting my golf bag. He's probably been around since this place was built."

Sarah flushed and chastised herself for opening her mouth and inserting her foot. She swallowed, attempting to dislodge the lump that crept into her throat. "Your concern is commendable, *Dr.* Collier."

Richard acknowledged the compliment with a nod but ignored her sarcastic tone.

Feeling more than a little unnerved by his presence in her room, Sarah directed her attention to the decor.

She supposed the oyster-colored walls and white wicker furniture were chosen to create an ambiance of peacefulness. But at the moment, tranquillity was far removed from the emotion she was experiencing.

"Does it meet with your approval?" Richard's voice, coming from just a few feet behind her, spread goosebumps down her arms.

"Yes, thank you," she answered stiffly without looking his way.

He walked to the French doors and parted the sheer, lacy panels. "Nice view."

"It certainly is."

"You have a balcony."

"How nice." Finding their forced conversation nearly unbearable, Sarah stepped closer to her suitcases. "If you don't mind, I'd like to unpack and take a long, warm bath. It's been quite a day."

"Of course." He gave a slight smile. "Will you join me later for dinner, say around nine?"

Sarah hesitated, then realized dinner would be the perfect opportunity to get things out in the open. She wanted to set a few ground rules right from the beginning. "All right," she said finally. "Nine it is."

Richard crossed the room. He hefted his golf bag onto his shoulder, then hooked a luggage handle with his index finger. With his free hand he opened one of the two connecting doors, then unlocked and opened the other. He paused long enough to give Sarah a brief smile. "I'll see you later."

After his door closed, Sarah quickly locked her own. She leaned against the dark wooden frame, pressed her palms to her singeing cheeks, then slid her fingers up to push her damp bangs from her forehead. She was a mess. The entire situation was a mess. How had she ever managed to fall head-first into her mother's trap?

She kicked off her shoes and felt the thickness of the luxurious pile carpeting under her feet. Slowly, she trudged over to the French doors and pushed them open. Through a grove of palms, she could see the vast splendor of the ocean. Far out on the horizon, she spotted the tall smoke stacks of a cruise ship silhouetted against the crimson sun that appeared to be slowly submerging into the Caribbean.

She felt like sinking too. What was she going to do?

Richard Collier wasn't her kind of man. Nor was she his type of woman. That much was obvious. What wasn't immediately obvious was how she could still enjoy a few days of vacation and avoid spending any time with her escort.

Chapter 3

Sarah turned this way and that before the full-length mirror on the bathroom door. A frown creased her forehead. Her gown, another token of affection from her mother, was black and had neat rows of sequins dancing down the sleeves. A deep slit on the left side exposed her slender calf. She wondered whatever possessed her to wear it. She was considering changing into her modest navy-and-white cotton dress when she heard a light tapping on the adjoining door.

"Too late now," she chided her reflection. She knew it was foolish for a woman of her age to be flustered by something as simple as a man accompanying her to dinner. But her moist palms and quivering knees were proof that she was more than a teeny bit nervous. She was petrified.

When she opened the door, her heart leapt to her throat. He wore a crisp, form-fitting light gray suit with a white oxford shirt and a silk tie of pewter, cranberry, and charcoal. She opened her mouth to speak, but no words formed. It was a disturbing, yet a rather wondrous feeling to know she would be sharing the evening with this handsome man.

"Good evening." Richard greeted Sarah with a smile as she stepped back to let him in.

"Hello, Richard," Sarah returned. A shiver rippled through her.

"You look lovely."

Caught off guard, Sarah's hands fluttered to her hair. "Thank you," she whispered.

He offered her his elbow. "I made reservations right here in the hotel at the Old World Lounge. The desk clerk assured me that the food is exceptional," he said as he opened the door leading to the hallway.

Ah yes, the eager-to-please woman behind the counter, Sarah thought, pursing her lips. She wouldn't be surprised if their cozy twosome became a crowded threesome by the time dessert was served. But then, why should she care?

In silence they rode the elevator down three floors to the mezzanine level. A hostess greeted them and led the way to a quiet, corner booth. The restaurant had a distinctive European flavor. The polished wood walls gleamed in the flicker of candlelight. The atmosphere was very subdued, very romantic.

Within seconds of being seated, a stunning blond cocktail waitress appeared beside their table. She smiled attentively at Richard. "Would you care for something from the bar?"

He gestured toward Sarah. "What's your preference?"

"Just some iced tea, please," Sarah said. She wasn't going to risk the dulling effects of alcohol on her senses when sharing the company of an admitted ladies' man. The more she thought of his occupation, the more her blood boiled.

"I'll have Scotch, neat." He spoke to the woman taking his order, but his eyes held Sarah's. "You don't need to be afraid of me," he whispered, after the waitress had gone. "I promise to be on my best behavior."

Sarah set her shoulders ramrod straight. "That's considerate of you," she replied with a biting touch of sarcasm.

Richard raked his hand through his hair. "Sarah, I'm not trying to provoke you or make you uncomfortable."

"I wonder if you have the faintest idea of how it feels to be utterly humiliated." After taking a glance into his cornflower blue eyes, Sarah took a deep breath and let her gaze move over his burnished mustache. Her shoulders drooped. "This is so embarrassing."

"What have I done to embarrass you, Sarah?"

"You wouldn't understand," Sarah said on a sigh. "Try me."

Sarah unfolded her napkin and meticulously placed each piece of her silverware side-by-side. How could she respond?

"Sarah?"

She kept her eyes focused on her hands and said, "Just being here with a man like you is . . . well . . . " She struggled for the right word. "It's awkward."

"Exactly what kind of a man do you think I am?"

Startled, Sarah stared at his stony expression. Had she hurt his feelings? She hadn't meant to. It hadn't even occurred to her that she could. Perplexed, she took a sip of water before trying to explain.

"Well?" he prompted.

"Well," she repeated, "you're outrageously charming and certainly good-looking—"

"Thank you."

Sarah narrowed her eyes. "And, I doubt you've ever had a lack of female companions. You probably have to beat women away with a stick!"

Richard winced. He'd had enough of this charade. Her erroneous assumptions were more than he could stand.

"I'm sorry if I've offended you, but given your profession, I—" Before she could continue, the cocktail waitress returned and very slowly, very gracefully set their drinks onto the table.

"I'll check back in a few minutes," the woman reassured Richard, then glided off in the direction of the bar.

Richard reached for his drink, took a swallow, then focused on Sarah once again. "We have to talk."

Embroiled in his own quandary, he locked his fingers around the glass until the tense muscles in his hand made him aware of his viselike grip. He lowered his glass onto the table with a muted thud.

"This whole thing was crazy from the beginning. I told Andora I didn't feel right about coming down here with you. But once she makes her mind up, a brick wall would be easier to reason with."

A waiter appeared and set a crystal bowl of shrimp cocktail in front of each of them. "Compliments of the hotel," he explained. His voice held a strong French accent. "My name is Jacques, and I am to be your waiter this evening. Would you care to see a wine list?"

Two heads turned in Jacques' direction. Two mouths voiced "no" in unison. Two heads pivoted back to their original position. Jacques laid the leather-bound menus on the edge of the table and hurried away.

Neither Sarah nor Richard touched their appetizers nor the menus.

"It sounds like you know my mother very well," she said, her tone cautious.

Richard inhaled a deep breath and let it out slowly. "I met Andora about two years ago. We both served on the committee to fund a new radiology lab at Children's Hospital."

"I see." Sarah lowered her chin and scowled at the linen napkin lying in her lap.

"No, you don't see." His voice was low and deceptively calm. "What I've been trying to tell you for the past ten minutes is that I'm not a gigolo or Casanova or whatever other label you've stuck to the middle of my forehead.''

Obviously confused, Sarah shook her head. ''Then what are you?''

He wasn't handling this well. So much for his keen intellect as a disciplined chess player, Richard mused. He picked up his glass and stared at the remaining drop of amber liquid. ''I'm a dentist. Just a man trying to earn an honest living.'' He raised his gaze to meet Sarah's and found her looking at him not with the hostility he anticipated, but instead with a bemused expression. Humor. It was the reaction he least expected.

Sarah laughed. ''Really? You don't say. And I'm a ballerina.''

''Somehow I don't think you believe me.''

''Why should I?''

''I'm a friend of Andora's. Don't you trust her?''

''Trust my mother?'' Sarah tried to keep her voice light, but failed despite her efforts. ''How well do you know my mother? Never mind.'' She held up her hand. ''I don't want to know.''

''Trust me, Sarah.'' He reached for her hand, but she pulled away.

''Richard, we both know who hired you. As long as we're together for the weekend, let's make the best of it, but let's not kid each other about who we are.''

''And who are you, Sarah?''

''Me? I'm a hard-working real estate agent who has

an important closing scheduled for tomorrow afternoon, a towering stack of appraisals waiting on my
desk, two out-of-town clients who need—''

''Whoa!'' Richard held up his hand. ''I'll tell you
what I think you are.''

By this time Sarah was intrigued by her most attractive dining escort. ''What?'' she asked.

''I think you're a very lovely young woman who's
forgotten how to have a good time—if you ever knew
how.''

Taken aback by his perceptive insight into her char-
acter, she blurted, ''If you had a mother like Andora
Trent Perkins Ballinger Thorndike Lavelle you'd be
leery of letting your guard down too.''

''Even in the short time I've known Andora, I can
honestly say she's the most eccentric woman I know,''
Richard admitted.

Sarah toyed with her water goblet. ''Truer words
were never spoken. I think somewhere in her family
tree she had an Auntie Mame.''

Richard raised his eyebrows. ''What do you mean
by that?''

''Haven't you ever watched the movie *Mame*?''

''Can't say that I have.''

Sarah took a sip of water. ''Mame is an eccentric
woman who lost her fortune but kept her flair for
living.''

''And she reminds you of your mother?'' Richard
asked.

''Most definitely! Especially when it comes to Mother's philosophy of life.''

''Which is?'' Richard prompted.

There was a long silence. She bit her lip, feeling like an idiot for sharing her analogy of her mother and Mame with a man like Richard. That was something private and personal that she'd never told anyone.

''Sarah?''

She looked into Richard's eyes and decided she might as well go ahead with it. ''Auntie Mame always said that life is a banquet and most poor fools are starving to death.''

Richard shrugged. ''Sounds basically true to me, but I take it you disagree.''

''I simply think,'' Sarah said distinctly, ''that if you eat everything at the banquet table, you'll make a hog out of yourself.''

Richard's deep spontaneous laughter caught the attention of the couples at the neighboring tables. ''I think getting to know you is going to be very interesting,'' he said with a grin.

Sarah turned her attention to the menu. Her case of nerves was spreading with the rampancy of dandelion seeds in a spring wind.

Richard drank the last drop of his fortifying Scotch. He set the glass down and leaned forward on his crossed arms. ''Tell me more about your mother,'' he said unexpectedly.

Sarah closed her menu and wondered how she could

avoid his request. "I hardly know where to begin," she answered. "Would you like some bread?" she asked, gesturing to the basket the waiter had placed on the table.

Richard nodded. He reached beneath the linen cloth and pulled out a dinner roll. "Would you rather talk about yourself?"

"No." Sarah tried unsuccessfully to slide a slab of frozen butter across her roll. To her dismay, it flipped from her knife and landed on the floor next to their table.

Richard retrieved it with his napkin, which was in turn swiftly removed from his hand by Jacques.

"I'll bring you some fresh butter," the waiter offered.

Sarah nodded her thanks. She tried not to dwell on how few times she'd been on an actual date. *Pretend it's a business dinner*, she told herself. Relax.

Fortunately, Jacques returned with additional butter and their dinners as well, precluding talk, at least for a while. Sarah hoped for time enough to compose herself.

"Have you lived in Michigan all your life?" Richard asked after a few minutes.

Sarah swallowed a nervous cough. "No, actually I was born in New York."

"What brought you to Michigan?"

"It's a long, long story," Sarah answered simply.

Richard smiled. "As they say, we've got all night."

Sarah cut a piece of her swordfish and dipped it into the sweet-and-sour sauce. "Growing up, I lived in ten different houses, in seven states." She took a bite of the fish.

"Is that why you became interested in real estate?" Richard asked.

Sarah nodded. His perception surprised her. No one else had ever made the connection between her interest in helping people relocate and her own nomadic life.

"I lived in one house all my life until I went to college," he continued. "When I graduated, I moved into an apartment, and that's where I still live. Moving around all the time must have been quite an adventure for you."

"I never really considered it an adventure—more like an experience to be endured," Sarah reflected.

"Where else have you lived?"

"California, Arizona, Florida." Sarah held up her hand and counted off the states on her fingers. "Vermont, Colorado, and of course, New York and Michigan."

"That's quite a tour."

"That's quite a life," Sarah countered. "We began moving after Dad was killed in a boating accident. Mother remarried a year later, and we packed up and headed for California."

"How long did you live there?"

"Nearly two years," Sarah answered. "We moved again the day before I was to have begun third grade.

One minute Mother and I were out buying crayons, scissors and notebook paper, and the next minute we were loading them into a moving van.''

At Richard's curious expression, Sarah continued. ''Fred Ballinger, Mother's second husband, had made his fortune in the dry-cleaning business and moved on to greener pastures.''

''He left?''

Sarah snapped her fingers. ''Just like that. And then it happened again a few years later.''

''Fred came back?''

''No, this time the fellow's name was Theodore Thorndike The Third. He was a real prize.'' Sarah shook her head at the memory.

''Somehow I think Andora's story is rather complicated,'' Richard observed.

Sarah nodded in agreement. ''My mother was an only child,'' she explained, her voice barely above a whisper. ''She was heiress to a fortune held in trust and doled out to her in a generous annual income. Ever hear of Trentco Paints?''

Richard nodded.

''Mother's maiden name was Trent.'' Sarah reached for another roll and broke it in half. ''My dad's family was equally wealthy. He owned several lumber yards in upstate New York. He died when I was five. Mother went through three more husbands in the next twelve years. Each of my stepfathers was distinguishably handsome, debonair, and deceptively broke. After

Mother foolishly bank-rolled each of their ventures, they took their share of community property and vanished with their fists curled around their stock certificates.''

Holding his fork suspended in midair above his baked potato, Richard listened intently to her story.

"I think Mother finally may have learned her lesson. Men still swarm around her, and she graciously accepts their attention, but she hasn't plunged head first into another marriage."

Richard shook his head. "You must've had quite a childhood." His voice was so gentle, so soothing. There was no condemnation, no accusation, just tenderness.

Sarah swallowed around the lump that had suddenly formed in her throat. "I never had a childhood," she said solemnly. "But I did learn some valuable lessons."

"And some painful ones too," Richard added.

"You're right," Sarah answered. "I used to pretend that we really lived in a big house by a lake and that we were just traveling from place to place. I used to dream that someday we'd go back home." There were tears in her eyes. She wasn't quite sure why, after all those years, old memories would return to haunt her now. What she did know, however, was that she didn't want Richard to see her cry.

Glancing around the room in an effort to clear her eyes, she saw that nearly all the tables were empty.

She checked her watch and was shocked to see it was almost eleven thirty.

"Would you like dessert?" Richard asked.

Sarah smiled and shook her head. "I couldn't eat another bite."

Richard signaled for Jacques to bring their tab, then helped Sarah from her chair. After signing the receipt, he took her arm and guided her toward the exit.

They stepped into the elevator and Richard took Sarah's hand into his. "I have a nine o'clock tee-off time tomorrow morning. Would you like to join me?"

The time had come for her to make a decision. "Richard," she began, focusing on the panel of buttons that lit with each passing floor. "I don't want you to feel obligated to spend time with me. I appreciate your offer but—"

"Do you have something else planned?"

"No, but—"

"Do you find my company repulsive?"

Sarah's lips twitched into a smile. "Not completely."

"Then I consider a friendly game of golf to be an appropriate activity for us, don't you?" He reached for a lock of her hair with his free hand and brushed it from her cheek.

"I didn't bring my clubs." The doors slid open and they walked down the dimly lit hall.

"Are you hinting I should increase your handicap?"

he teased, keeping her right hand tucked snugly into his left one.

"No." She looked directly into his eyes. "I don't want to take advantage of you."

They came to her room, and she stood facing him. When Richard took a step closer, Sarah pressed her back against the door. The coolness of the wood seeped through her dress.

"I'd like to get to know you better," Richard said. He placed his hands lightly on her shoulders, his touch flooding her with a sudden, inexplicable warmth.

Sarah took a deep breath. "I don't think that's a good idea."

"Why not?"

Sarah felt her knees quiver. She'd better say something and fast. She took a quick gulp of air. Before she could think of an appropriate reply, he lowered his mouth to hers.

Her head grew light, swimming with the sweet sensation, all sense and sanity draining to her toes. It had been a long time since a man had kissed her. She felt her breath catch in her throat. The kiss was slow and gentle, yet her senses were swirling and her pulse racing.

Gradually, their lips parted. His arms remained loosely wrapped around her as if he didn't want to completely let her go.

"When will you be ready?" he asked.

She frowned and her eyes filled with confusion. "Ready for what?"

"Golf," he whispered, his breath moist and warm against her cheek.

"Golf," she repeated, immensely relieved that she had misinterpreted his question. "I'll be ready by eight-thirty."

Richard smiled. "I'll meet you in the coffee shop. Of course, I'll have eaten by then, so if you want breakfast, you'll need to get up earlier."

Sarah groaned. He was also a morning person. Just her luck. Forcing a slight smile, she opened the door and retreated to the quiet solitude of room 437.

Chapter 4

Sarah's wake-up call came precisely at seven. She rolled to her side, lifted the phone from its cradle and moaned. Morning wasn't her favorite time of day. She loved to experience the relaxed, unencumbered state that only sleep could provide. Sleeping in was a luxury she couldn't often afford.

After a few seconds of careful stretching, she rubbed her eyes, crawled out of bed and padded into the bathroom.

Following a quick shower, she pulled a white, gauzy blouse and a pair of royal blue shorts from the top layer of clothes in her suitcase. The glowing red digits on the clock radio told her that she had a half hour to spare. Another thirty minutes she could have spent sleeping, she thought grimly. She ambled back into the bathroom and brushed her hair, pulling it back at the temples and securing it with delicate gold combs.

A streak of sunlight sliced through the narrow opening between the drapery panels, beckoning her to the French doors. She pulled back the heavy brocade drapes, parted the lacy sheers, raised her arms far above her head, and stretched in the morning sun. Then, without a second thought, she opened the door and walked out onto the balcony. She closed her eyes and lifted her face to the breeze.

For the first time since she'd arrived, she smelled the special aroma of the island. Fresh in the morning's first light, it was a blend of sand and salt and lush tropical verdancy, a bouquet evoking lavish thoughts of laziness and leisure.

She looked down at the stone walkway that threaded its way through a grove of palms to a canopied verandah. Flower gardens bordered the grounds of the hotel, each plot carefully landscaped according to the color and height of the blooms. The mountains rose in magnificence above the tops of the trees, adding a majestic background to an already splendiferous scene.

A few minutes later, when Sarah entered the coffee shop at the Silver Sands, she was delighted by the bright, elegantly spacious room that overlooked the pool on one side and the aquamarine waters of the Caribbean on the other. Colorful yellow and blue umbrellas were scattered randomly on the sandy beach. They shaded a handful of early risers lounging near the surf. The morning sun poured through the floor-to-ceiling windows, reflecting off the silver cutlery and crystal goblets on each table.

Sarah spied Richard, a copy of the Wall Street Journal occupying his hands, seated at a table with an ocean view.

"Well, good morning," he exclaimed, putting down the paper and rising to his feet. He helped Sarah into her chair, then returned to his.

Richard's snug, tan Bermuda shorts and nutmeg-colored golf shirt emphasized the exceptional muscle tone of his arms and legs. His neatly combed hair was still damp from the shower, and his face was smooth and ruddy from his morning shave.

Sarah inhaled the spicy scent of his cologne and thought he looked better now than he had the night before, if that were possible. And if there was one thing she didn't need, it was a man, particularly this man, looking so darned appealing that it nearly took her breath away at eight o'clock in the morning.

She confronted him with a grave expression. "I called the office this morning. The secretary told me that during the night at least a foot of snow fell." She took a sip of coffee. "My closing's been canceled. My partner's teenagers are complaining that every time there's a decent snow it's always on a Saturday, so they never get a day off school."

Richard laughed. "I remember feeling the same way a few years ago. It's nice to know kids still have their priorities straight." He gestured to the window. "And today my top priority is shooting par for eighteen spectacular holes."

"Do you golf often?"

Again Richard chuckled. "If I didn't play every Wednesday afternoon during the season, I'd risk being kicked out of the American Dental Association. Actually, during college I considered turning pro, but my buddy Jack convinced me that he'd make a much better partner in a dental practice than he would as a golf caddie.''

''You really are a dentist, aren't you?''

His eyes twinkled. ''That's what it says on my diploma.''

''And did Jack become your partner?''

''He sure did. We've been together since the eighth grade. At times like this I really appreciate him.'' Richard caught Sarah's questioning expression. ''Old Jack had to dig his way to the office this morning, while I have the pleasure of basking in the sunny Caribbean, and sharing your company.'' His smile widened.

Sarah felt her cheeks grow warm and brought a glass of ice water to her parched lips. His eyes were on her. Even without actually watching him, she knew they were. She felt her blush spread over her neck and throat.

She was immensely relieved when a waiter appeared to take their order.

After they finished their breakfast of warm cheese croissants, fresh fruit, and coffee, Richard took Sarah's arm and escorted her to a waiting taxi. He grinned at her as he opened the cab door.

She settled onto the seat, feeling her pulse rate accelerate as Richard slid in next to her, his long, bare legs brushing hers. She wished she hadn't worn shorts; wished she hadn't agreed to go with him this morning.

"Where are your clubs?" she asked, remembering their destination.

Richard leaned back into the seat and smiled. "They're cleaned and polished and waiting for me at the first tee." He let out a long sigh and extended his arm along the length of the backseat. "All part of the superior service rendered at the Silver Sands."

Sarah nodded. A shiver tingled up her spine as Richard's hand rested on her left shoulder. It felt good, very good, to be sitting this close to him. Her eyelids drifted closed as an unfamiliar weakness crept over her. His scent, his nearness, surrounded her, and she had absolutely no desire to be anywhere other than right where she was.

All too soon, she lurched forward as the cab stopped abruptly at the canopied entrance to the Mullet Bay Clubhouse.

Richard stooped and set the ball on the tee. He stepped back and took a few practice swings, then addressed the ball, sending it into a perfect arc against the brilliant blue sky. With the club still poised over his shoulder, he watched the tiny white speck bounce then roll to a stop on the thick grassy carpet of the fairway, less than thirty feet short of the green.

"Perfect shot," Sarah said, casting him a wary glance. He was totally relaxed and in control, and she felt like a family of butterflies was having a reunion in her stomach. She approached the tee and took a deep breath. Her limited ability at golf would soon be all too apparent.

By the third hole, Sarah could barely endure her embarrassment. Never known for grace or agility, she was certainly outdoing herself today. She had managed to slice, chop and hack away at the ball, sending it in every direction except toward the flapping flag that taunted her from the green.

She wondered if Richard would be satisfied to play only nine holes, but since he was shooting close to par, he gave every indication that he planned to play all eighteen. And why shouldn't he? After all, this was his vacation, and he was entitled to enjoy himself. But how much enjoyment could he have teamed up with the Incredible Klutz? The thought was depressing.

Sarah slammed her driver into the pale pink rented golf bag and walked toward the back of the tee. Richard was getting ready to swing. Another beautiful shot, straight as an arrow, right down the middle of the fairway.

When Sarah faced the ball at the fourth hole, she tried to clear her mind and concentrate. However, as she swung, she lost her grip, and the club slid through her clammy hands.

Miraculously, she still made contact with the ball. It sliced to the right, ending up in the rough on the edge of the fairway.

"Another perfect shot," she mumbled, tromping over to a marshy area near a clump of trees in search of her ball. Her sneakers made a squishing sound as she stepped into a pool of tide water that had trickled its way over the sandbar. Frustrated by her wet, sloshing feet and the deliberately uncooperative little white ball, she began to use her club to poke through the tall grass.

"Having trouble?" a deep voice asked from behind her.

She whirled around. Richard was standing only a few feet away.

"I think it landed farther down, near those bushes," he remarked, gesturing to a sloping incline about twenty feet from where she was looking.

Sarah put her hands on her hips and watched him walk to the exact spot that her ball had rolled. She looked thoughtfully up at the sky. It wasn't enough that she had no control over the ball. She couldn't even remember the general direction she'd sent it.

Richard pulled a towel from his bag and wiped the murky water from Sarah's ball. "Here you are," he said softly, placing the cold, dimpled sphere into Sarah's outstretched hand. "Ready to face the sand trap on the fifth hole?"

Sarah forced a smile and nodded, all the while her mind screamed *Nooooo*.

They waited in silence on a redwood bench for the couple who had previously followed them to tee-up and send their balls soaring through the air. Sarah could easily guess that Richard had suggested that the older gentlemen play through when she had made her pilgrimage into the rough.

Slowly, Sarah approached the women's tee. She bent her head and stared at her clubs, pretending to choose one for her next shot. Finally she reached into her golf bag and pulled the head cover from the driver.

"Would you like me to show you where you went wrong?" Richard took a step closer, placing his hands lightly on her arms.

Sarah froze, afraid to move. She felt color surge to her cheeks. When his large hands enfolded hers on the grip of the clubs, she started to tremble. The world receded, taken over by Richard Collier's presence.

"Now pay close attention," he instructed. His breath was warm in her ear as he spoke. "Keep your head down and follow through, like this." His hands guided her arms back in a gentle practice swing. Her heart was riveting like a jackhammer. Taking a deep steadying breath, she willed herself to relax and wished that her fair skin didn't betray her embarrassment so easily. She felt as if her cheeks were burning.

This man was as dangerous as a live grenade, she thought to herself as she nibbled her bottom lip. Her conscience reminded her she should put her feet in gear and move out of his reach. But her heart willed her feet to stay rooted where they were planted, right between Richard's pair of golf spikes.

His hand came up to brush her cheek, then he leaned forward to drop a soft kiss on the nape of her neck. ''On with the lessons,'' he said, removing his arm from her shoulder. His eyes twinkled mischievously as he waited for her to tee off.

By the eighteenth hole, Sarah had hit her stride. She had successfully managed to avoid the water hazards and sand traps and felt a surge of renewed energy. She swung easily, lofting the ball gently onto the fairway.

''Hey, who taught you to play golf like that?'' Richard teased after rewarding her with a round of applause.

Sarah smiled. ''I've been taking private lessons from a pro.''

Richard stroked her cheek with the backs of his knuckles. ''You know, Sarah, your whole face lights up when you smile. You should do it more often.''

He was impossible to dislike, she decided. She liked his courtesy, his intelligence, his sparkling sense of humor, his engaging grin. In fact, there was very little that she didn't like about him.

That could complicate matters. How could she convince herself to avoid a man who was difficult to resist?

At two-thirty that afternoon, Sarah walked down the stone steps to the beach. It was crowded with sun-worshippers. She found a pair of empty lounge chairs a few feet from the Silver Sands cabana bar, where Richard had agreed to meet her, and sat down.

A hotel attendant handed her two towels, then adjusted the angle of the striped umbrella to shade her already pink-tinged skin from the powerful rays of the tropical sun. Before she could settle into a more comfortable position, she spotted Richard heading toward her. From her vantage point she watched his languid approach and felt a powerful wave of anticipation wash over her.

Sarah's eyes narrowed in annoyance when a sleek, young woman waved her arms and ran up to Richard. From the looks of her golden tan, she was no stranger to the beach scene. She approached him with feline grace, until she stood within inches of Richard's towering frame.

"Hi, I'm Danielle, but my friends call me Danni." Her words drifted on the wind, and Sarah eavesdropped. "I'm on my way to the bar. Want to come with me?"

Sarah strained to hear Richard's response above the spray of the nearby surf. To her amazement, she saw him gesture in her direction.

"No thanks, Danielle. Someone's waiting for me."

"Too bad," the girl drawled. "Maybe some other time." She raised her arm and carelessly draped a white beach coat over her shoulders.

Obviously another member of the Richard Collier fan club, Sarah thought. Apparently women were attracted to him like flies to flypaper.

Yet, she hadn't seen him encourage them. Maybe he had so many others waiting for him at home that he wasn't interested in a vacation fling. Whatever the reason, Sarah was comforted to know that her escort wouldn't make a fool of himself—or her—by chasing every girl who threw herself at him.

Richard sat on the lounge chair next to Sarah's, then slipped off his shirt. A scowl creased his brow. "Did you see that teenager come up to me?"

Sarah nodded.

"One false move and I could've been arrested for contributing to the delinquency of a minor. I'd like to see as much of St. Maarten as I can, but the inside of the local jail isn't on my list of attractions."

Sarah couldn't resist the temptation to tease him. "I guess I'll have to protect you from all these shameless women," she said, straightening her shoulders.

Richard seemed to measure Sarah's petite form. "What more could I ask for?" he said with a smile. "I like a woman who takes matters into her own hands. How about escorting me into the water?"

Sarah laughed but shook her head. "I need to stay in the shade until I build up my tan. My skin burns easily."

"So does mine, but that clear water is too tempting to pass up."

Sarah watched him walk through the sand into the surf and then slip under the surface of the aquamarine water. With his powerful arms, he stroked through the breaking waves. Moments later, he emerged from the sea, his wet skin gleaming in the bright sunlight. Within seconds he stood next to her again.

''Water's perfect,'' he said breathlessly, raking both hands through his hair. He spread out his towel on the lounge and lay on his back, his eyes closed, his hands folded beneath his head.

She knew better than to openly stare at him. But . . . he was so handsome . . . and the temptation was too strong.

Sarah rummaged through her canvas tote bag in search of her oversized tortoise-shell sunglasses. With her eyes shielded by the dark lenses, she surreptitiously examined Dr. Collier.

A breeze swept through his honey-blond hair. His lower lip was full under his bushy mustache. Her eyes traveled to his firmly muscled chest and flat stomach then back up to his wide shoulders. Suddenly her mouth was as dry as the sand. If anything, she had underrated his appeal. He exuded health, vitality, and a maleness that sent her pulse into orbit.

Then, to her embarrassment, he glanced around and caught her staring at him. Her face burned with the inevitable blush she had never been able to control. What was wrong with her, mooning like a schoolgirl? It was unnerving, to say the least, to act like this. She had to stop this errant attraction which threatened to overtake her whenever she happened to be in Richard's company.

How lasting was temporary insanity? she wondered.

Wasn't reality supposed to kick in when hot sunlight melted the mysterious spell of darkness?

Her stomach rumbled and, in its own way, her heart did too. Or maybe it was her pride in subtle protest. Whatever the cause, she needed to put some distance between herself and Richard Collier.

She sat up and wiggled her toes in the hot, smooth sand, undecided as to her next move. Should she retreat to her room, or walk along the beach until she found something cool to drink? She pushed her glasses to the top of her head, squinted against the penetrating rays of the sun, and headed to the closest bar for a lemonade.

As she walked back to her chair twenty minutes later, two bikini-clad women strolled by her. Both had flowing blond hair parted in the middle, both were wearing swimwear that left little to the imagination, and both were eyeing Richard. Even though his eyes remained closed, Sarah sensed that he was wide awake.

She watched with interest as the girls stopped inches from Richard's feet. The taller one, wearing a shimmering gold suit, bent down and peered under the edge of the umbrella. "Excuse me," she said, removing her mirrored sunglasses.

Richard opened one eye, rolled to his side, and propped up on his elbow. "Hmmmm?"

"My friends and I are getting a volleyball game together and we need a couple more players. Would you and your," she looked at Sarah, "your friend like to join us?" She flashed him a brilliant smile. Her white teeth sparkled in contrast to her deeply bronzed skin.

Richard sat up and looked at Sarah, who offered him a lemonade. "How about it? Would you like to play volleyball?"

Sarah wanted to decline. She hadn't played volleyball since physical education class in junior high school. But the enthusiasm in Richard's voice warned her that if she didn't play, she'd spend the rest of the afternoon sitting alone. And suddenly she had no desire to be by herself. She nodded and managed a slight smile.

"We'll be there in a few minutes," Richard assured the girls.

Sarah pulled a brush and a red banana clip from her tote. She scooped her hair into a thick pony tail, then turned to face Richard. "I think it's only fair to warn you that I haven't played a lot of volleyball."

He grinned, looking happy and carefree. "I'm bound to be rusty too. It's probably been over a year since I've played."

"That long?" She felt more ancient by the minute. With a sigh of frustration, she dug through her totebag for her sunscreen.

An hour and a half later her strained hand muscles cried for mercy, but her young, energetic team members continued to volley valiantly in an effort to break the tied score of two games each. One game would have been more than enough for her.

A spontaneous cheer echoed around her.

"Way to go, big guy," someone yelled from behind her. Richard had scored another point. She was lucky to make contact with the ball, and Richard was popping the ball over the net one time after another. She wiped the beads of sweat from her forehead with the back of her hand. Sand clung to her damp skin. She felt grimy, dehydrated, and exhausted.

"Your serve," Richard called, tossing the ball to her. "Take your time. This is the game point."

"No pressure here," Sarah mumbled as she balanced the gritty ball on her left palm. She straightened her shoulders and took a swing. The ball plopped into the sand two feet in front of her.

"The net's a little higher than that, honey," a stocky man beside her coached. She gave him a cool stare. Her next swing sent the ball smack into the back of the unsuspecting girl in front of her.

"New server," an irritated voice demanded.

"Give her another chance. She's just getting warmed up," Richard said in her defense.

"It's a little late for that," someone returned with a laugh.

It's a little late in more ways than one, Sarah thought. Who was she kidding? It was at least ninety degrees and she couldn't remember ever being so hot. Her hair was plastered to her head and her fingers felt numb. She mustered enough strength for a final wallop of the ball. This time, to her amazement, the ball floated over the net. The other team immediately shot it back to Richard's waiting hands. With a mighty blow, he scored the winning point.

"It's party time," the gold-clad blond announced. Sarah watched as the group ran in the direction of the bar. They were actually *running*, Sarah observed, still rooted to her spot. She barely had strength enough to crawl back to her chair, much less sprint across the beach like a gazelle. Maybe she should start taking vitamins, or maybe the inevitability of old age was just creeping up on her.

There it was again. Why did she always think of herself as being so old? Those other girls couldn't have been more than five or six years younger than herself. Had she been that active five years ago? Five years ago seemed like another lifetime. A time when she had David. . . .

"You look like you're ready to pass out," Richard said when he reached her side. "Are you feeling okay?"

"Am I still standing?" Sarah responded with a weak smile.

Richard chuckled, then without warning scooped her up into his arms.

"Richard!" she shrieked. "Put me down."

"No way," he laughed.

Sarah squirmed in protest when she realized his intention. He planned to toss her into the water!

Chapter 5

"You wouldn't dare!" Sarah shrieked.

"Oh, wouldn't I?" Richard gave her a mischievous smile and kept on walking.

Seconds later, she felt the cool water of the ocean cover her feet and legs. A wave broke over their heads, and Sarah slipped from his grasp. She dove into the water and swam away from shore.

After a few strokes, she treaded water and with shaking fingers, pushed her wet hair from her face. Her eyes stung from the salt and the intense glare reflected off the water. "You're just lucky I know how to swim," she sputtered after catching her breath.

"I would've saved you."

"Says the man who tried to drown me."

Richard grinned, then sank beneath the surface for a minute, tossing his head with a flourish when he came up.

"I think you're starting to burn," Sarah observed.

"Yes, Mother," he retorted. "Want to race me to the shore?"

"I don't know if I can make it that far," Sarah answered.

"You know what they call the last one in," Richard teased. With that he dove under the water. Sarah was right behind him.

When they reached the beach, she was out of breath. The air burned in her lungs, but deep inside she felt great. She hadn't had this much fun in a long, long time. She felt young and alive. For the first time in years, she felt free of the responsibilities of being a real estate saleswoman or a home owner or a bill payer. She didn't have a care in the world and it felt fabulous.

"You're a good swimmer," Richard commented as they gingerly stepped over the rocky sandbar that bordered the beach.

"I think all the salt in the water held me up and floated me along," Sarah returned.

Richard laughed and reached for her hand.

He had the most open, honest laugh she'd ever heard. It came from deep inside him, a spontaneous, hearty sound. Sarah playfully swung her hand linked with his. She felt an exultant urge to laugh with him.

When they reached their umbrella, Sarah smoothed her rumpled towel and stretched out on her stomach. The warm breeze whispering over her cool skin caused her to shiver.

Seconds later, she closed her eyes and let the soothing rhythm of the waves lull her. Succumbing to a pleasant languor, she smiled. The small sigh she gave was one of utter contentment.

She so seldom relaxed anymore. There was always so much to occupy her mind, most of it related to work; people to phone, appointments to keep, records to check at the county zoning office, loan officers who had to be reminded to fulfill contract deadlines. When she wasn't actually doing real estate work, she was thinking about it.

A glance over at Richard revealed that he was lost in his own thoughts. What could he be thinking about? she wondered. He was certainly given to being quiet for long stretches. She noticed that he had changed positions. He was no longer spread out on his back. Now he sat cross-legged on the edge of his towel, and he was staring directly at her.

"Hi," he said. His voice was light, lazy.

"Hi." Sarah felt her pulse accelerate when his mouth curved in an appreciative grin. She rolled onto her side to face him, then reached up and brushed her bangs away from her forehead.

"Is something bothering you?" Richard asked.

"No, why?"

"You've sighed at least a dozen times in the last fifteen minutes. I thought something might be on your mind."

Sarah flushed with his astute observation. Wordlessly, she bowed her head, hiding her face with her hair.

Richard stood and wiped off some of the sand from the bottom of his foot. "The crowd's starting to thin out. Would you like to go for a walk?"

She took a breath, caught herself before she emitted another sigh, then raised her eyes to meet his. He gave her a smile that sent her heart racing.

Before she spoke she moistened her lips with the tip of her tongue. "Now that I've had a chance to catch my breath, I'd love to hunt for some shells."

"That sounds good to me." He gestured toward the foam spreading onto the beach. "I haven't taken a single picture since I've arrived. Tomorrow I'll bring my camera."

"Not to take pictures of me, I hope." A grim expression crept onto her face.

Richard chuckled and reached for her hand, gently pulling her to her feet. "Actually, photography's my hobby, and I'd like to try out my wide-angle lens on some seascapes."

Sarah smiled, content that his interest was in nature and not her. She stooped to pick up her totebag and made sure all her belongings were inside.

"If you let me toss in my shirt, I'll carry the bag."

Sarah quickly handed the bag to him. "Who could pass up an offer like that?"

Richard curled the fingers of his left hand around the bag's thin canvas straps, then offered his right hand to Sarah, his fingers interlocking with hers.

Sarah walked beside him, chiding herself for the

tingle of excitement she felt. Ahead of them stretched a panorama of pink sand, coral cliffs, and the incredible azure blue of the ocean that frothed onto the beach like a rich layer of meringue. The air smelled of the powerful blend of salt and sea. Sarah's eyes devoured it, her lungs drank it in. She wiggled her toes in the superfine granules, squished forward several steps, then wiggled her toes some more.

Without lifting her gaze she began to speak. "Richard, there's something I've got to ask you."

He slowed his pace. "Ask anything you like, Sarah."

She cleared her throat and kicked at an incoming wave. "Do you have a girlfriend?"

"If I did, I wouldn't be here," Richard answered quietly.

She looked at him for a long moment.

"How about you?" he asked.

"How about me, what?"

"Do you have someone waiting at home?"

"I don't date."

"Not ever?"

"No."

The finality of her proclamation caused Richard to stop in his tracks. "Don't you ever get lonely?"

Sarah turned to face him. "With my business and all of my clients constantly around me?"

"That's not what I meant."

"Of course I get lonely," she confessed, lowering her lashes to conceal her eyes.

Richard raised her chin with the tip of his thumb. Her eyes locked into his gaze. "Then why don't you do something about it?"

"I value my independence."

"So do I, but that doesn't mean I can't enjoy a social life as well."

"Relationships complicate things," Sarah countered.

"Not all relationships turn out as badly as your mother's."

Sarah nodded. "I know."

"Why don't you give us men a chance to redeem ourselves? We're not all snakes."

"Are you suggesting I hire a dating service?"

"No. I'm suggesting you start spending some time with me."

Sarah's mouth went dry, and she swallowed to ease the sudden tightness in her throat as she absorbed the impact of his words. He wanted to continue seeing her after they returned to Michigan. That was something she certainly hadn't anticipated. Weekend vacations were . . . well, they were vacations. Life at home was reality. Sarah wondered if she would ever be emotionally prepared to have a relationship with another man.

She'd already had her chance at love. Real love. Didn't that special kind of magic only happen once in a lifetime? It had for her mother. As hard as Andora had tried to recreate that special bond with husband after husband, none could compare with Sarah's father. And it would be the same for Sarah herself.

Sarah dug her toes into the sand and looked at the long stretch of hotels threading their way along the beach. Finally, she managed to speak. "I don't think that would be a good idea."

The totebag slid from Richard's fingers. He rested his hands on her shoulders and looked directly into her eyes. "Why not?"

Sarah met his gaze, afraid that her eyes revealed her emotions. She was mesmerized by the sincerity in his expressive blue eyes. As if suspended in time, they faced each other. The only movement was the gentle tide that quietly immersed the tops of their bare feet with warm water.

She stared at him for what seemed like an eternity, then looked away.

"I want to spend time with you," he said softly.

Sarah could feel her resistance melting. Why were her barriers breaking down now? she wondered. Something had changed. Alarms were discharging throughout her mind. Her carefully structured existence had been her source of protection.

She'd simply refuse to be tempted to surrender her heart. How difficult could it be to just politely tell him no? Who was she trying to kid? She could already feel her defenses beginning to crumble.

"Sarah." He spoke her name like a murmured caress then cupped her face with both of his hands and lowered his mouth to hers.

His warm and tangy lips tasted of salt. His tantalizing mustache tickled her skin. She reveled in his embrace.

Slowly their lips drifted apart. Breathless, Sarah took deep gulps of the balmy air as if she'd been running in a marathon. She leaned her forehead against his chest.

Richard kissed the top of her head. "I don't know about you, but all this exercise has given me an appetite. Where would you like to go for dinner?"

Sarah pulled from his embrace and rocked back on her heels. "I feel like going to the most ridiculously expensive place on the island."

Richard's eyes narrowed. "Why?"

"Since my mother obviously intended for us to enjoy ourselves, I think we should put her money to good use."

"What makes you think Andora's paying for this trip?" Richard was suddenly serious.

Sarah swallowed. "Isn't she?"

Richard shook his head. "No," he answered flatly.

For a moment Sarah could only stare at him, unsure of how to interpret his blunt answer. It finally became clear to her. "You mean you . . . you're paying for all of this?" She dropped her arms in amazement.

A broad smile lit his face. "That's right. I tried to tell you last night, but you wouldn't listen."

His nearness was suddenly intimidating. He towered over her, standing within an arm's length, his eyes narrowed slightly as if monitoring her reaction.

Sarah's mind began to whirl. She was seeing the entire situation between him and herself in the light of this new knowledge and was rapidly working her way toward being indignant.

"Why didn't you tell me right away, when we were on the plane? Why did you let me believe you . . . you were something you weren't?"

His shoulders moved in a slight shrug that spoke the same gesture of apology as his faint smile. "I guess I started enjoying the fact that you mistook me for a playboy. People normally regard me as being serious and conservative, and it felt good to slip into the role of somebody else for a while."

"At my expense," Sarah said angrily. "I hope you thoroughly enjoyed your little charade." Not wanting to continue the conversation, she grabbed her bag from the sand and took off at a brisk pace in the direction of the hotel.

"Wait a minute!" Richard called.

An arm came around her waist, stopping her in her tracks. It also made her breath catch in her throat. She wished fervently that this man would not feel at liberty to put his hands on her.

"I think it's time we cleared up a few more things." He eyed her intently, then released her arm and stepped back. "Do you still think your mother paid me to accompany you?"

"I, uh . . . . Well, yes. What else am I supposed to think? My mother arranged for me to take this trip, then you showed up as part of the package."

"Sarah, that wasn't the way it happened. That's what I've been trying to tell you." Richard took a deep breath. "I was part of a bachelor-for-rent auction to raise money for the children's hospital. Your mother bid on me. Her money went into purchasing oncology equipment. I pledged to take the highest bidder on an all-expense paid trip down here, but your mother said you would go in her place."

Sarah stared at him, her eyes round and challenging. Astonishment had replaced anger. "You're not going to pay for *my* expenses! Whether you realize it or not, I do have some pride. From now on, we'll split the expenses fifty-fifty." She paused for a breath and her gaze rested on his mouth. Her brow furrowed. "What are you grinning at?"

"You." He leaned forward and brushed her face with his knuckle. "You're beautiful when you're angry."

Sarah groaned and rolled her eyes heavenward. "Flattery will get you exactly nowhere with me, Dr. Collier. It only makes me suspicious."

He arched an eyebrow. "What are you suspicious of?"

How should she respond? She still didn't trust him

wholly, and she didn't trust herself, either. How could she tell him the real reasons? His attention, his kindness, his beguiling laughter were the reasons she was deliberately keeping her distance in spite of their being together.

How could she explain that whenever he touched her even in the most casual manner, he seemed to cast a spell over her. She could barely breathe, much less talk. Yet, she felt herself being drawn closer and closer to him with each passing second.

''Well?'' he prompted, continuing to stare at her.

''Maybe I suspect you're too good to be true,'' she responded finally.

Richard nodded and stroked his chin thoughtfully. ''I've noticed something else about you, Sarah.'' He said each word softly and distinctly. A ghost of a smile hovered under his mustache.

Sarah tilted up her chin. ''What else?'' she asked, interested in his comments despite herself.

While pretending to study her, he gently clasped her head and turned it from side to side. ''One side of you is reserved, refined, controlled. But the other side . . . '' He let out a long low whistle. ''You've got a stubborn streak a mile wide. And unless I miss my guess, when you get angry, people would be wise to evacuate the area.'' He raised both brows. ''Am I right?''

''Close enough,'' she conceded, all too aware that he'd cleverly distracted her from the issue of money. ''What about dinner?''

He leaned closer. Sarah could see the thickness and length of his sandy lashes, feel his warm breath fanning her cheek. A grin crinkled the skin around his eyes.

"Actually, I'm starving, and I was hoping you'd offer to treat."

Sarah nodded, her heart stopping between beats. Twenty-four hours ago she wanted nothing to do with him. Now she'd agreed to buy his dinner. She really was slipping over the edge.

"We've walked quite a distance," Richard remarked. He turned around and offered his hand to Sarah. She ignored the gesture, pretending to adjust her sunglasses. "Our hotel is a fair hike away," he continued. "Would you like to stop for a drink along the way?"

"No thanks," Sarah said. The last thing she wanted to do was prolong the afternoon. The second to the last thing she wanted to do was talk about herself. Before he asked her another question, she'd be smart to direct the conversation elsewhere.

"So, what do you do when you're not on the bachelor auction block?" she ventured, trying to keep her voice light.

Richard raised a brow. "Have you decided I'm not a gigolo after all?"

"I'll give you the benefit of the doubt," she replied.

"I told you last night. I'm a dentist."

Sarah stopped walking. So did Richard. She narrowed her eyes in a quick appraisal. "You just don't look like a dentist."

"Oh? What should a dentist look like?"

Sarah shrugged and picked up her pace again. "Older, I guess. Bald, maybe. More . . . well . . . married." she could feel the heat rushing to color her cheeks. Why couldn't she simply have kept her mouth shut instead of attempting conversation?

"My Uncle John is a dentist. He's older, and bald, and married, too. But I never thought of those qualities being a prerequisite for working on people's teeth. None of my patients have ever complained that I'm not older or—"

"All right!" Sarah interjected. "I apologize. I'm sorry that I've insulted you."

Richard slowed his pace considerably, causing Sarah to stop for him to catch up with her. His head was downcast. She'd made him feel badly again. She hadn't meant to offend him. How could she make amends?

"It must have been flattering to have all those women bidding on you during the auction," she said in an attempt to boost his obviously deflated spirits.

He gave her an odd look. "On the contrary. It was rather insulting, actually."

"If you disliked the idea so much, why did you agree to participate?"

"Who said anything about agreeing? Your mother didn't exactly ask me."

"Oh?" Sarah looked at him inquiringly.

"I volunteered to help Andora plan the auction. I had no intention of offering my services as an eligible bachelor."

Sarah nodded her understanding. "She bamboozled you."

"Correct," Richard enthused. "Sarah, would you mind stopping for a minute?" He gestured to his foot. "I think I stepped on a piece of coral, and my toe is bleeding." He plopped onto the sand.

Sarah knelt and reached out spontaneously to touch his foot in a purely sympathetic gesture. He turned his head slowly to look up at her and her fingers trembled slightly against his smooth skin.

Realizing what she was doing, she drew her hand away as though she'd been stung. Drawing a deep, steadying breath, she stood, then took a few steps back, trying to put more space between them. For several long, nerve-stretching moments Richard merely sat and watched her.

"I—" Sarah gulped, her voice failing her, her heart hammering in her ears. "I'm sorry you're hurt." She swallowed again. "I should have noticed that you were limping." In an attempt to do something productive, she rummaged through her bag and pulled out a tissue. "Here, wrap this around it."

"I, uh, think it may be better to rinse the sand off first."

"Right. I'll go get some water." She had only walked a few yards when she spotted a discarded paper cup lying next to a sand castle. She quickly walked to the water's edge, rinsed the cup as well as she could, and filled it to the rim.

"Thanks," came a deep voice from directly behind her.

Startled, Sarah's hand shook causing most of the water to slosh from the cup. "Richard! I thought you were still back there. Should you be walking on that toe?"

"I should unless you plan on carrying me back to the hotel."

Sarah rolled her eyes.

"The cut isn't as bad as it looks. It's just a superficial skin wound. After I clean it, you probably won't even be able to tell where it was."

Sarah refilled the cup and handed it to Richard. He promptly doused his foot. "There. Almost as good as new," he proclaimed.

"Does it still hurt?" Sarah asked.

Richard shook his head. "Not much, but I think we'll need to alter our plans for the evening."

"Oh? Were you planning to eat with your feet?"

"No, but I was considering dancing on them. A trip to the Caribbean wouldn't seem complete without dancing to Calypso music. Don't you agree?"

Sarah shrugged, thankful she wouldn't have to experience an evening of being held in Richard's arms. Forgetting him and erasing all the beautiful memories would be difficult enough without adding another dimension. The whole weekend was snowballing from a simple vacation into . . . into . . . well, it was all getting far too complicated.

Richard Collier was too attractive, too potently magnetic, and she had a light-headed feeling whenever she got too close to him. She felt like she'd fallen into a whirlpool of out-of-control emotions.

And another evening spent in his company was yet to come.

Chapter 6

The evening that followed was unexpectedly delightful for Sarah. The weather continued to be glorious, allowing them to dine on the terrace beneath a canopy of stars.

To her surprise, Sarah found herself laughing a lot. She was different, here, now. How much was due to Richard's influence? she wondered. Was it the effect he had on her or was it merely that she was on vacation? She tried to tell herself it was the latter, that she was happy and relaxed because of her surroundings, that her spirits were high because of the sunshine and balmy temperature. But try as she might, Sarah couldn't quite convince herself she would have been equally contented if she had traveled alone.

Richard was nothing like the man she had thought him to be, the man she'd been so angry with, so set against from the start. She had already developed a sneaking regard for him, something more than merely liking him. She had grown to respect him. If she was looking for male companionship, and she kept reassuring herself she was not, but if she were . . . Richard definitely . . . .

Sarah didn't sleep very well that night. As she lay in the darkness trying to analyze the evening, conclusions just weren't there. Nothing made sense.

She tossed and turned until, finally around three o'clock, she ventured outside to sit alone on her balcony in the quiet Caribbean starlight. She attempted to occupy her thoughts with anything other than those which immediately sprang to mind. But, it was impossible.

For a while, she sat watching the ocean, gazing into the rolling, moonlit waves that softly broke on the deserted silver beach. A gentle breeze had developed, a warm, restful wind that blew hazy strands of clouds across the creamy full moon. After she'd watched the moon climb higher and higher, she closed her eyes and willed herself to relax. Peace of mind eluded her.

She went back into her hotel room and climbed in bed. Giving the pillow a firm punch, she decided she simply had to put things into perspective. Suddenly her head was full of unanswered questions.

Her feelings for Richard were . . . different . . . unique. How clearly she remembered the way his wind-tossed hair invited her to run her fingers through it, the way his spicy cologne tempted her to snuggle closer to him, the way his low, masculine voice caused her insides to vibrate with nervous awareness.

Finally, in the quiet stillness just before dawn, Sarah

admitted to herself that she was falling in love with Richard Collier.

She felt angry yet elated at the same time. One part of her wanted to shrink back into the past without a single memory of the present. Another part wanted the joyous feelings of anticipation to last without being shattered by the intrusion of reality.

Her world was spinning, tumbling, whirling around like a balloon in a tornado. Her thoughts became more and more jumbled until at last sleep rewarded her with a temporary repose.

The next morning Sarah met Richard for a leisurely, late breakfast, then they spent a few hours browsing around the shops in town. Richard had already used several rolls of film, as he kept asking Sarah to pose by anything and everything he thought might make a good picture.

"Richard!" she protested. "I thought you liked landscapes! Haven't you run out of film yet?"

"Nope." He focused and snapped a shot of Sarah sitting on a stone bench, the ocean to her back.

"You've taken dozens of pictures today. What are you going to do with all of them?"

"I'll probably develop them, sort through them and put the best ones in an album," he told her. "Now, turn the other way, with your face toward the sun."

Sarah sighed, but scooted to a different position while he clicked away. She noticed an older gentleman wearing a tropical print shirt who was walking toward them.

"Why don't you sit down there with your wife, and I'll get a picture of the two of you?" the man asked, gesturing to Sarah.

"Thanks!" Richard responded eagerly, handing over his camera.

"Put your arm around her," the man prompted. "Act like you know her."

Richard did just that.

The sheer absurdity of the situation caused Sarah to smile just as the shutter clicked. Richard retrieved his camera and thanked the man, who turned and walked away with a smile and a wave.

"Richard! Why did you let him think we were married?" Sarah asked as they began to head in the direction of the Silver Sands Hotel.

"I was only protecting your honor," Richard said, stopping for a moment to secure his lens cap.

"You were *what*?"

"Protecting your honor," he repeated. "Think about it, Sarah. Would you have rather I corrected the man's assumption and explained that we aren't married, but merely vacationing together in paradise?"

Sarah drew in a long, startled breath and willed herself not to blush. He was right! Why hadn't she thought of that? "Thank you," she said as graciously as she could.

Richard grinned. "You're most welcome. It's not

often I get to slip into my knight-in-shining-armor mode.''

Sarah smiled back, feeling light-hearted again for some strange reason. She glanced at her watch. Their plane departed in less than four hours. They'd barely have enough time to eat lunch and pack before heading to the airport. Where had the weekend gone? Where had her sanity gone?

Richard reached for her hand and linked his fingers through hers. He was such a special man. He deserved a special woman. But sadly, Sarah knew she wasn't that woman. She had carefully created an independent life for herself, one she was sure would provide for her basic needs and keep her heart scrupulously guarded.

In time she would get over Richard. And it was far better to start the healing process now, rather than to wait until she got to the point where she couldn't live without him.

They continued to walk toward the hotel, hand-in-hand, the tropical sun warming their skin and the lush rustle of breeze-stirred palms serenading them.

''How about some lunch?'' Richard asked after several conversationless minutes. ''We could eat outside. It'll be quite a while before we can do that in Michigan. So we'd better enjoy it now.''

Sarah smiled as she caught a glimpse of the waves rolling up on a nearby beach. ''You're right. Let's eat by the water.''

He guided her along a stone path and approached a hostess who stood at the entrance to a charming outdoor cafe with terraces facing the ocean.

An hour later they had finished their lunch and were sipping frothy pineapple coconut drinks at a small wrought-iron table beneath a lightly flapping umbrella. Sarah turned her face to the beautiful azure sky and drew in a breath of clean, fresh air. She didn't want the afternoon to end.

She looked down at her hands folded in her lap, and realized that by midnight she'd be back in Michigan. Alone. She'd been alone for so much of her life—why should that prospect disturb her now? She felt safe in her oneness, didn't she?

"Sarah?" Richard asked gently, pulling her from her reverie.

"Yes?" she murmured.

He regarded her with interest. His gaze lingered on her face so long, she felt warmth rising to her cheeks. Casually, he reached across the table and lifted her right hand. He turned it over as if examining it, stroking her palm carefully with his forefinger. A shiver rippled down her spine.

"We're friends, aren't we, Sarah?" he queried finally.

Sarah nodded.

"Then I don't understand why we shouldn't continue to enjoy each other's company."

She didn't understand herself. Why didn't she go

ahead and tell him she wanted to see him again? Why not, when he obviously enjoyed being with her as much as she liked being with him?

The answer came immediately; because she would get emotionally involved, that was why. To some extent she already was. Somehow, she had already surrendered her heart. And it scared her to pieces.

Love had sneaked up on her when she wasn't looking. How, when, why, she didn't know. It just had. She had to put up more barriers, had to make it clear she had no intention of becoming romantically attached to anyone. There was no way she could afford to lose control of her emotions again.

As calmly as she could, she took a deep breath and tried to convince herself she had always told him the truth and was going to remain truthful. "Richard, I'm content with my life just as it is. I have a good job. I keep busy. I have total freedom in every sense, and that's the lifestyle I want."

He waited until she'd finished, his expression one of dubiousness mixed with puzzlement, and released her hand. "I'm content too, Sarah. So, what's your point? What does your job have to do with our spending time together?"

"Nothing . . . no, everything. Richard, it's so confusing, I can't explain it. Please don't ask me to try."

"Sarah," he said, reaching for her hand again, "I don't want to let you go. If I didn't care about you, it would be easy for me to accept your attitude as a brush off, but I do care about you. About us.''

Us? Panic rose in Sarah's throat. He considered them to be a couple?

He must have interpreted the fear on her face. ''Is it that you still don't trust me? Your opinion of me hasn't changed, has it? All this time we've spent together and you *still* believe I'm a womanizer.''

''No! I don't think that at all!'' Sarah groaned. ''Oh, Richard, you've been a perfect gentleman, and I've had a very special weekend that I'll always remember.''

He was listening keenly, his eyes not leaving hers. When she'd finished talking, he said, ''If you don't think I'm some kind of an ogre, then why won't you agree to see me again? What you've said doesn't make any sense. Now, suppose you tell me what you really mean.''

Sarah knew Richard deserved an explanation. He was genuine and honest, more so than any man she had ever met. And that scared her. At this point, she even scared herself.

She guessed she'd better say something before her mind ceased to function. ''There hasn't been a man in my life for a long time,'' she began. ''That's the way I like it.''

''Why?'' His expression of genuine astonishment made her feel desirable. For some reason, the fact that he could cause these stirrings in her put her on guard.

In the face of her silence, very gently, he went on. "What are you afraid of, Sarah? Please tell me."

Sarah turned away, choking back the emotion that threatened to burst from her. She took several deep breaths before she spoke.

"I was engaged once," she said, her voice barely above a whisper.

"And?" Richard urged.

Sarah lifted her face and once again their eyes locked. "And . . . my fiancé died."

Richard tenderly squeezed her hand. "I'm sorry, Sarah. I had no idea."

"I met David my junior year at Michigan State. We were both studying business administration and had a lot of classes together. We dated steadily for two years and planned to get married as soon as we graduated. He bought me a ring, I'd picked out a dress, everything was set." The words seemed to spill from her lips on their own accord.

"David accepted a job with a consulting firm in Indianapolis, and while he was driving home from apartment hunting one Sunday afternoon, he stopped at a convenience store." She paused only briefly to gasp a breath before continuing. "A gunman was in the process of robbing the place. When David walked in the man panicked. David was shot in the chest and died instantly."

A sorrowful expression settled on Richard's features. He propped his elbows on the table, steepled his fingers, and closed his eyes. Finally, after several moments, he focused his gaze once again on Sarah.

"Did you have any family or friends to help you get through it?"

Sarah lifted her shoulders then lowered them with a sigh. "Mother was on an Alaskan cruise when it happened. She got home as quickly as possible. And . . . and I guess I never really had any close friends. I always knew a lot of people, but because we moved so much it was hard for me to make lasting friendships. David was my best friend. You just can't imagine how abandoned I felt."

"Yes, I can," he murmured almost to himself but just loud enough for Sarah to hear.

"Did you . . . have you . . . ?" she struggled, not knowing how to ask the awkward question.

Richard nodded. "I know all about losing someone you love," he told her. "My sister died of leukemia when she was twelve. I was sixteen. She was sick for so long, in so much pain." His eyes clouded, and his voice roughened. "I never felt such helplessness in my life as I did when my parents told me Beth had died. My beautiful little sister died before she had a chance to live."

Alone in his thoughts, he remained silent for a long time.

"That's why you volunteer at the Children's Hospital, isn't it?" Sarah asked quietly.

Richard nodded. "I still miss Beth terribly, but I

know now that life has to go on. My first reaction was to quit the football team, stop seeing my friends, and in general keep myself barricaded upstairs in my bedroom. I'd probably still be up there if my dad hadn't talked some sense into me.''

"What did he say?'' Sarah ventured.

"He told me he'd lost two of his children. There was nothing he could do to bring Beth back, but he refused to watch me waste my life. He prodded and nagged me until I started showing up for football practice again. He called my friends and encouraged them to include me in their plans. He even rented a cabin at Higgins Lake and took my best friend Jack and me ice fishing.''

"Your father sounds like a wonderful guy.''

"He is,'' Richard confirmed. "He's taught me a lot, and probably the biggest lesson was that you can't keep yourself locked up in a state of self-exile when problems come along.''

Sarah nodded mutely.

"Do you really understand, Sarah?''

"Yes, why?''

He didn't have to say what was on his mind. She could guess the reason for that frown of disapproval creasing his brow. Richard shifted impatiently in his chair and raked a hand through his hair. "Things change in our lives sometimes, and we can't control them.''

"I'm aware of that.''

"You may be aware, but I'm not convinced—"

Sarah interrupted him with a loud sigh of exasperation. "Richard, what I do or don't do isn't really any of your concern."

"Think about what you're saying. You can't hide from reality, Sarah."

His voice had taken on such a stern quality, Sarah felt as if he were reprimanding her. She straightened her back defensively. "I hardly keep myself confined."

"Oh yes you do, at least emotionally," he insisted. "You admitted you spend all of your time at work. If that isn't confining yourself, I don't know what is."

"I have to support myself, and sometimes that means putting in long hours."

"There's nothing wrong with working for your own personal satisfaction. Ideally, everyone should have a rewarding job. But when it starts to take precedence over everything else, something's wrong. You're hiding, Sarah."

"I am not," she retorted, irritated to the core.

Richard slapped his palm down on the table with a loud thwack. "Prove it! Say you'll go out with me. I don't care where, you name it. The theater, dinner, a Pistons game, a concert. Anywhere."

Sarah thought twice before replying. She didn't want to obligate herself to something she had no intention of doing. On the other hand, she didn't want to hurt Richard's feelings when he was obviously making an attempt to do for her what his father had done for him.

"That's a tempting offer." Oh, so tempting, she thought. "But, I can't accept," she said carefully. "You're a terrific man, but I've already explained I don't want any sort of romantic involvement at this point in my life."

"Neither do I," he said unexpectedly. "And to prevent the possibility of future misunderstanding, maybe I ought to clarify another point. I'm not looking for a wife." With that he pushed his chair from the table and stood. "And, since you've made it perfectly clear that you don't want my company . . . ''

Spots of color flamed her cheeks. "I'm sorry, Richard," she whispered.

"No sorrier than I am," he replied tersely.

Sarah followed him across the patio and he paid for their lunch.

"Would you like to share a cab to the airport?" he asked.

"Of course. I'll be ready in a half hour," Sarah replied, his formal tone making her feel isolated again, as she had before their weekend. It distressed her even more to realize how much lonelier she felt now.

"Fine. I'll meet you in the lobby."

Silently they walked through the hotel and rode the elevator to the fourth floor.

*   *   *

Later they hardly exchanged a dozen words in the taxi. Sarah kept looking out the window, staring at the beautiful resorts, the lush landscape, remembering all she had seen and done with Richard.

As she boarded the small commuter plane for San Juan, she breathed a final farewell to the sunlight glittering around her and struggled to maintain her composure. The last thing she wanted was to do what she was on the brink of doing—bursting into tears.

She tried to sleep on the long flight from Puerto Rico to Michigan, but found it impossible. Richard occupied not only the seat next to hers, but her thoughts and her heart as well.

It wasn't until the plane was circling the Detroit Metropolitan Airport that the first hot tear slid down her cheek. She tried to tell herself she was being affected by the idea of freezing weather. She could see the snow thickly blanketing the surrounding fields as the plane made its final descent. But it wasn't just her thoughts about the weather. The prospect of being back home wasn't particularly uplifting.

Resentfully, illogically, she blamed Richard for making her so depressed. If only he hadn't brought excitement into her life. Now, even the thought of getting back to work, which used to be more than enough to keep her happy, saddened her.

It would pass, she decided resolutely. All she had to do was keep thoughts of Richard from her mind.

Once she was back in her old routine, she'd be the enthusiastic career woman she used to be.

They got off the plane, retrieved their luggage, rode a shuttle to the parking lot, and located Richard's BMW. Sarah got into the car while Richard scraped snow and ice from the windows.

Nothing was said on the way to Sarah's house. There didn't seem to be anything to say. Sarah couldn't have explained her feelings if someone had paid her to try. They were jumbled. She wanted to spend time with Richard Collier more than she had ever wanted anything else in her entire life. But, something was stopping her from telling him so.

Another driver cut in front of them and Richard had to slam on his brakes to avoid a collision. The tranquillity of paradise was far removed from them now. Reality had returned. Her capacity for reasoning would soon follow suit, wouldn't it?

In less than twenty minutes, they pulled into her driveway. ''Looks like someone shoveled your walk,'' Richard commented as he turned off the motor.

''The teenager who lives next door does it in exchange for help with his algebra,'' Sarah provided.

Richard looked at her curiously. ''So you know your neighbors?''

''Of course,'' Sarah replied, wondering where he was steering the conversation. She almost hated to ask, but found herself doing it anyway. ''Why?''

"It surprises me. You seem like the type who would prefer not to be bothered with outsiders."

Sarah sighed and opened her car door. He must think her a real recluse. What other conclusions had he drawn about her? Why did it matter so much?

He carried her bags up the walk and waited for her to unlock the front door. When she had, he set her luggage inside and extended his hand to her. His fingers were cold, but Sarah nonetheless felt a rush of warmth from the contact.

"Have a good life, Sarah Perkins. And don't be too hard on Andora."

Sarah nodded, plagued with sorrow when he released her palm. She couldn't watch him walk away. With a muffled sob, she shut the door. Her house felt strangely inhospitable, as though it had been uninhabited for months instead of only a weekend.

She took off her coat and tossed it haphazardly onto the back of the couch. Not bothering to turn on any lights, she gathered up her belongings and stumbled up the stairs toward her bedroom. Once there, she collapsed on the bed and gave in to the empty sadness wracking her soul.

Chapter 7

T he next day began with a flurry of activity. Sarah arrived at the office earlier than anyone else and sorted through a mountain of paperwork. Before eleven o'clock she had returned a dozen phone calls and shown a client she'd been working with for several weeks three homes that had come on the market over the weekend. Because of their floor plans, none proved suitable, however, and Sarah promised to check into additional listings.

She had just taken a bite of the apple she'd brought for her lunch when Evelyn Ferguson, Bradley's wife and their receptionist, knocked on the glass partition that separated Sarah's office from the other agents'.

Sarah glanced up and smiled at the motherly looking gray-haired woman.

"You're back!" Evelyn exclaimed, walking into the wood-paneled room. "And just look at that tan. Did you have a good time?"

Sarah nodded unenthusiastically. "Has anyone called the National Bank for today's mortgage rates?"

she asked while making herself a note to call her mother.

"The figures are in your box. And Bradley wants to see you. He'll be back in the office after three."

Sarah stopped writing and looked up at Evelyn. "Is something wrong?"

"I'll say there is," Evelyn retorted. "Charlotte Knox paid us a visit last Friday. She wants to leave Gateway Realty and come over to Middletown."

"What!" Sarah shrieked, scarcely believing the news.

Evelyn nodded and continued. "Since you went to certification school with her, Bradley wants your opinion on whether to take her or not." Evelyn wrinkled up her nose in a gesture of disgust. "If you ask me, that little floozy is nothing but trouble."

Sarah couldn't have agreed more, but she kept her thoughts to herself. "Have you seen her sales figures for the last quarter?" she asked.

Evelyn sighed. "Are you kidding? She fanned them in front of Bradley's face the minute she arrived. They're impressive, as usual. She's been Gateway's top agent for the past two years. And Bradley says high-pressure, obnoxious agents can't sell houses. Hah!"

"Perhaps they can sell 'houses', Evelyn, but I doubt that they can sell 'homes,' " Sarah said.

"How right you are," Evelyn agreed. "Speaking of homes, the Flannerys called and are interested in talking to a few custom builders. They'd like you to set up some appointments.''

Sarah opened a file cabinet and pulled out a manila folder. "Oh yes, the Flannerys," she said, scanning their information sheet. "I thought they'd probably be more satisfied with a custom home. It says here they need a minimum of six bedrooms. Now, let's see, where did I put those architects' brochures?''

''You're the most efficient person I know,'' Evelyn commented as she headed toward the door. "I'm going down to the delicatessen. Can I bring you a chicken-salad sandwich or anything?''

''No thanks,'' Sarah replied, tossing the remains of her apple into the trashcan. "I've had lunch, and I'll be leaving in a few minutes to list another property.''

Evelyn shook her head. "At this pace, by the end of the week you'll need another vacation.''

If Charlotte Knox came to work for her, she'd need more than a vacation, Sarah thought with a groan. Evelyn's description of "floozy" was too kind. Charlotte was the type of agent who gave a bad name to the profession. She was like a dog with a bone. Once a potential customer acted even remotely interested in listing or buying, Charlotte sank her teeth into them and refused to let go. The woman didn't know the meaning of the word ethical.

Sarah penciled *Meet With Bradley* in the four o'clock slot of her daily planner. Charlotte Knox was one complication she didn't need on her first day back.

After driving over the snow-packed streets for nearly a half hour in heavy traffic, Sarah finally reached the home of an elderly lady whose husband had recently passed away. The woman had explained to Sarah on the phone that she knew she couldn't keep up the large suburban house. She hated the idea of selling it, but didn't know what else to do.

Sarah chatted with the woman for quite a while, patiently answering all of her questions. When her client seemed more comfortable with the situation, Sarah went on a tour of the house. She took careful measurements and listed the features of each room as she listened to the woman relate stories of happier times.

"Oh, I hope I can find a condo big enough for my furniture but small enough for me to take care of by myself," she fretted aloud as she poured cups of tea for herself and Sarah.

Sarah slipped the tape measure back into her purse and joined her client at her kitchen table. She patted the woman's hand. "I'm sure we'll get a very good price for this home, Mrs. McCoy. And I know of several brand new condos within just a couple of miles from here. It might be easier for you to stay in this neighborhood since you're familiar with the shopping, and most of your friends probably live here."

A broad smile lit Mrs. McCoy's wrinkled face. "Do you really think I can find something close? I just had it in my head that I'd have to pack up and move clear across town.''

"We have lots of options right in your own backyard. Would you like to start looking tomorrow afternoon?'' Sarah asked.

"That would be nice, dear. I'm glad my friend Ethel Parson recommended you. She was very pleased that you sold her home so quickly and found her such a nice new place.''

Sarah smiled. "Ethel had a lovely home, and she had another advantage too. She put her house on the market in the spring, when many people start thinking about relocating. Since we still have a foot of snow on the ground, it may take us a little longer to find the right buyer for your house, but I'll put an advertisement in tomorrow's paper to get things started.'' She drank the last sip of her tea and stood.

Mrs. McCoy also rose and led Sarah back into the living room. "I appreciate your being honest with me. I guess I don't need to tell you that I've never had to deal with this type of thing before.'' She parted her sheer curtains and stared outside. A worried frown creased her brow, and she drew in a deep breath and let out a long sigh. "Will you need to put one of those signs in my yard now?''

"It's up to you,'' Sarah told her. "I can if you like, but if you'd rather, I could advertise in other ways.''

"Could you?'' the older woman said in obvious

relief. "I sit here by the front window and look out a lot, and just thinking about that sign . . . well. . . . "

"I know how you feel," Sarah soothed. "I moved around quite a bit when I was a child, and I always had to tell the other kids that I lived in the house with the *For Sale* sign in the yard. It depressed me too." She put on her coat and gloves. "I'll be back tomorrow around three," she said, opening the front door.

As Sarah walked her to Ford Bronco parked at the curb, she noticed Mrs. McCoy standing at the window waving good-bye. Sarah waved back and gave her the "thumbs up" sign. Elderly clients always received her special attention. Sarah knew from experience how disturbing and unsettling an unwelcome move could be. She did everything possible to take care of her customers and to ensure that their relocating process was as painless as possible.

Back at her office, Sarah had just enough time to phone the newspaper and place an ad for Mrs. McCoy before meeting with her partner.

Bradley Ferguson was a sensible, solid businessman in his early sixties. Sarah respected him a great deal. He'd given her the option to buy into his company a few months ago when he was recovering from a mild heart attack. It was then he'd decided to spend more time with Evelyn, his two daughters, and his five grandchildren, and less time managing other agents and selling homes.

Sarah knocked softly on his door before entering.

Bradley was seated at his desk and smiled when he saw her.

"Sarah! I haven't seen much of you since you've been back. Come in and sit down. It looks like you've had a long day."

She sank into a smooth leather chair. "Mondays are usually hectic. Did everything run smoothly while I was gone?"

Bradley nodded while lighting his pipe. "The big snow slowed things down. We even closed at noon on Saturday."

"Evelyn tells me someone is interested in joining our ranks."

Bradley nodded, his expression guarded. "Charlotte Knox." He puffed his pipe for a few seconds before speaking again. "I don't mind telling you I have some real reservations about her. I've spent the better part of my life and all of my career establishing Middletown Realty as a reputable agency. Charlotte sells houses, but her methods . . . " He emitted a low whistle.

"Then let's not offer her a position," Sarah suggested.

"Unfortunately, it's not as simple as that. With Bill retiring last Christmas and Lois moving to Colorado, that leaves us a little understaffed."

Sarah perched on the edge of her chair. "I can pick up the slack, Bradley. I'm willing to work longer hours until someone suitable comes along."

"That's just it. You already do the work of three

people." He flipped through a binder of computer printouts on the corner of his desk. "Sales for the last quarter were up by eighteen percent citywide. Our agency had an increase of only seven percent. Our competitors are getting the listings. We need a couple of extra agents and we need them now."

"But do we need Charlotte?"

Bradley rubbed his brow. "It's a tough call. My first inclination is to bring her onboard with stipulations." He counted them out on his fingers. "All of her contracts must be approved by either you or me. We'll encourage her to, uh, adhere to our dress code."

He cleared his throat then took another puff on his pipe. "Some of those leather skirts she wears . . . well, we'll just have to strongly suggest she dress appropriately. And, at least initially, her floor duty will be on Tuesdays and Wednesdays when we're less busy. In other words, we'll watchdog her."

"It sounds like you've put a lot of thought into this," Sarah said.

Bradley nodded. "I have."

"Then I'm willing to give her a try if you are," Sarah replied.

"I think she's our best option at this point. So, I'll call her first thing tomorrow morning," Bradley offered.

The word "call" triggered Sarah's memory. "If there's nothing else, I need to phone someone too," she said as she stood.

"Nothing else except try to get some rest."

"I just came back from vacation," she called over her shoulder.

Upon returning to her own office, Sarah closed the door and immediately dialed a familiar seven-digit number. A lilting feminine voice answered on the first ring.

"Mother, how could you?"

"Sarah! You're back! Did you have a nice time?"

Sarah twisted the phone cord in her fingers. "I repeat, how could you?"

"How could I what, dear?"

"You know perfectly well what I mean, so quit using that innocent voice," Sarah scolded. "Some mother you are, practically throwing me at a man. Whatever possessed you to plan that trip?"

"I liked the location, and I liked the man," Andora replied simply.

Sarah rolled her eyes to the ceiling. "Great! I might have known."

"Don't you like him?" Andora countered.

"What's not to like? He's charming, intelligent, handsome—"

"Splendid! So, you'll be spending more time with him?"

"No, I won't, so you'd better stop your plotting," she told her mother. "I don't need complications in my life."

"I'll agree that you don't need 'complications', but

you do need someone to pluck you out of that deep, dark well of an existence you've thrown yourself into," Andora protested. "Now tell me what you did together in St. Maarten."

"There really isn't anything to tell. We ate and went to the beach. After all, I was there with a perfect stranger." But even after she said the words, she knew it wasn't quite true, though it should have been. She'd felt an odd sense of knowing him, or having known Richard for a long, long time.

"Sometimes being with a 'perfect stranger' is better than vacationing with someone you know. Did the two of you get along?"

"I guess," Sarah said noncommittally.

"Then, why don't you call and invite him over for a meal. Bachelors love home-cooked food, and you make a wonderful beef stroganoff."

Sarah sighed and swiveled in her chair. She caught a glimpse of a poor withering potted plant on top of her file cabinet. She didn't even have time to water her plants, let alone entertain a man. "I'm too busy to add anything else to my life right now."

"Nonsense! You've got to make the time. You have so much love to share, but somehow you've forgotten how. You need someone with the strength and patience to reach the real Sarah you keep hidden deep inside."

Sarah swallowed and felt a burning in the back of her throat.

"I want so much for you," her mother continued

quietly. "I want you to experience the marvelous feelings that come from sharing your love with a special man. Your father and I had that kind of relationship."

Sarah fought to suppress her tears. She tried to speak, but choked on the words. Taking a deep breath, she whispered, "I'm not ready, Mom."

"I think you are, Sarah, but I won't prod you any further. Just promise me that you'll think about what I've told you."

"I will."

"Good. Did you remember I'm leaving for Europe tomorrow?"

"Tomorrow? I thought you weren't going until sometime later this month."

"Yes, well that's all changed."

How like her mother to alter plans at the last minute, Sarah thought.

"When I get back, let's get together for dinner. Instead of staying two weeks, I'll only be gone for six days. Can you pencil me into your schedule for Thursday night next week, or will you be working with a client?"

Sarah consulted her calendar. "I don't have any plans for that evening."

"Perfect. There's something important I need to discuss with you, but it will keep for a week. I'll see you at seven, and I'll bring some Chinese food. You can make the tea. We'll have a quiet little visit at your house."

Sarah agreed and replaced the receiver. What could her mother possibly want to talk about? Whatever it was, Sarah knew from experience to brace herself for the unexpected.

During the next few days, Sarah was too busy to devote more than an occasional thought to Richard. Usually the first week of February was a slow period in her business, but this year proved otherwise.

It was Sarah's experience that most people seemed to think that real estate brokers merely showed houses every once in a while and collected huge commissions on other agents' sales. Sarah's job was far more complicated than that.

The previous November, one of her part-time agents had sold a house but neglected to do a thorough title search. The closing of the sale still hadn't taken place because a former owner had an outstanding lien against the property. Since that owner had sold the house himself, without the assistance of a realtor, the new owner was none the wiser. Now he knew better, but not before he had signed a contract stipulating that he would vacate the house in thirty days.

A month later the new owners had their furniture shipped to Michigan from Georgia and had nowhere to put it. The seller couldn't move until he had his money from the sale. Sarah had spent the entire holiday season trying to negotiate a compromise.

The entire situation had snowballed into a complicated legal affair. Because the listing agent had since left Middletown Realty, both the seller and the buyer phoned Sarah daily, demanding that she solve the problem. She, in turn, called the law firm handling the case.

If that predicament wasn't enough to deal with, she was also working with a husband and wife who were relocating from California. Since theirs was a mandated corporate move, neither were thrilled with the prospect of leaving the sunny Pacific. Sarah had shown them dozens of homes, none of which met their specifications. The biggest challenge of all was their requirement of a large outdoor pool and cabana, not a popular feature of northern homes.

On Friday morning Sarah conducted the usual sales meeting and directed the tour of new homes listed during the week, including Mrs. McCoy's. That afternoon she showed the California couple several more places, one of which sparked a flicker of enthusiasm. Located in Forest Glen Estates, the newest and most expensive development in the area, the house had an expansive backyard, including a tennis court and pool.

Later that evening, back in her office, Sarah sat at her desk waiting for an agent from another company to return her call. She massaged the tired muscles in her neck and shoulders with one hand and jotted down a series of notes with the other hand.

"Sarah, you look different today," came an unexpected male voice.

Startled, Sarah jumped and looked up from the papers spread on her desk. "Bradley! I didn't realize you'd come back in."

"Evelyn and I were passing the office on our way home from dinner, and I remembered a file I needed for a meeting in the morning. How long are you going to work tonight?"

Sarah shrugged. "I don't know, another fifteen minutes maybe." She reached for her mug and finished the last sips of lukewarm coffee.

Bradley clicked his tongue. "You're working too hard." He looked at Sarah thoughtfully for a long moment, then said, "You're wearing a new outfit. That's what's different. Did Andora buy it for your birthday?"

Sarah nearly choked. If only her mother would have been satisfied to just buy her a suit. "No," she replied. "I went to the mall last night and decided to treat myself to something new."

"Good for you," Bradley said and then left, closing the door softly behind him.

Alone in her office, Sarah turned back to her paperwork. But her mind wasn't on it. For an instant, the office faded away completely, and she could see Richard's face, hear his voice, feel the warmth of his mouth on hers, as surely as if she was back in St. Maarten, in his arms.

She shook her head, trying to dislodge the memories.

In spite of all the distractions and frustrations, today she had been thinking about him almost constantly.

She glanced at her watch and was surprised to discover that it was nearly seven-thirty, much later than she had intended to stay. If she left right away she'd make it home in time to catch up on some laundry and go to sleep at her usual time, just after the eleven o'clock news. Then she remembered a trip to the store was necessary if she intended to eat breakfast in the morning. A conscientious notemaker, she pulled a grocery list from her purse and added cereal and laundry detergent.

She turned on her answering machine and just as she rose from her desk, ready to leave, Evelyn called over the intercom. ''Sarah, someone is waiting for you in the lobby.''

Sarah gazed down at her daily planner. No appointments were scheduled for the evening. Had she forgotten to write something down?

''Should I send him back to your office?'' Evelyn asked.

''No, I'll come out,'' Sarah returned. She slipped on her suit jacket for a more professional image and quickly ran her fingers through her hair in an attempt to look her best.

She stepped from her office into the hallway and stopped in her tracks. It was impossible. It was insane. It was Richard.

She swallowed hard, her heart fluttering like a trapped dove in her chest at the sight of him. She took a deep breath and tried to squash down the gladness that kept welling up inside her.

Dressed in a navy pin-striped suit and a crisp white shirt accented by a red and navy tie, he looked wonderful. If anything, his appeal was stronger and more compelling than ever. Taken off guard, Sarah couldn't hide her blush of pleasure. She felt unsteady when she walked toward him and he offered her his hand.

"Hello, Sarah."

"Richard, what a surprise!" She congratulated herself on being able to speak.

"Dr. Collier, do you know my esteemed partner?" Bradley piped in as he joined his wife in the lobby.

"We've golfed together," Richard returned with a bright smile, causing Evelyn's brows to rise.

"Sarah golfed? Recently?" she asked.

Richard turned to Sarah. "A week ago, wasn't it?"

All she could do at that point was nod.

"Last week!" Evelyn exclaimed. "Why, that must mean you were together in St. Maarten."

"No wonder you look different, Sarah," Bradley added with a wink. "Why didn't you tell us there was a man in your life?"

Not knowing quite how to answer, Sarah gnawed her bottom lip.

When Richard responded with, "She isn't used to the idea yet," Sarah wanted the floor to swallow her. The last thing she wanted was rumors to circulate around the office about her. Especially absurd false-hoods that didn't remotely resemble the truth.

"As it happens, though," Richard continued, "to-night I'm here to see Sarah for strictly professional reasons."

"Oh?" Sarah said, at once suspicious of his motives.

Richard looked directly at her and nodded. "I want to buy a house."

Chapter 8

"**Y**ou *what*!" Sarah exclaimed, utterly shocked by his nonchalant declaration.

He gave her a winning smile. "A house," he repeated. "You do help people buy houses, don't you?"

"Yes . . . yes . . . but . . . "

"Sarah is one of the best brokers in the city," Bradley boasted. "She'll find exactly what you're looking for."

"I have a great deal of confidence in her too," Richard said.

"Well," Bradley said, helping Evelyn on with her coat, "we'll leave you two here to discuss the preliminaries." He shook hands with Richard. "Good to see you again, Dr. Collier."

Sarah waited until Bradley and Evelyn were outside before she turned to face Richard. "Okay, why are you really here?"

"I told you. I want to buy a house."

Exasperated, Sarah planted her hands firmly on her hips. "People don't just waltz in here late at night and announce they want a house."

110

"Why not? Isn't this a real estate office?"

"Of course it is, but . . . are you sure you're serious?"

"I'm serious," he said and gave her a crooked smile.

That smile again, Sarah thought. She had to develop some defense against it, or the entire situation could get quickly out of control. Richard Collier was positively lethal!

He motioned for her to precede him, and she led the way to her office. Seconds later they were seated on either side of the desk, facing each other.

"What should I do first?" Richard asked.

"Quit smiling at me!" Sarah practically shrieked, then regretted the words when she saw his brows knit together in a deep frown.

"Should I scowl?"

His response brought a slight smile to her lips.

"That's much better, Sarah."

His smooth, deep voice saying her name took all the resistance out of her. His tone washed over her with nerve-honing awareness, and the memory of the weekend before flooded back to her. She felt his gaze move over her, and knew by the expression in his eyes that he was remembering too.

Sarah tried to catch her breath. She could scarcely believe Richard was actually sitting in her office, that he wanted to buy a house. "Are you sure you really want—"

"When a prospective customer walks in here, do you usually try to persuade him to change his mind?"

Sarah shook her head.

Richard grinned. "You look great, by the way. You got your hair cut, didn't you?"

Sarah nodded and self-consciously ran her fingers through her newly styled hair. "Just a few inches. I thought, uh, I guess I just wanted to try something different." How like him to try to throw her off track. He merely smiled at her and leaned back in his chair.

She glared at him. He looked innocent.

"Look, Sarah, maybe I shouldn't have come. I sincerely want to protect my investments, and I've researched the housing market enough to know that mortgage rates are low and house prices are stable. In my estimation this is a good time to buy. Now, if you don't want my business—"

"I didn't say that."

"Not in so many words, but—"

"Richard, this may not be as easy as you think. Choosing a home is a major commitment."

He smiled suddenly. "I'm ready to make a commitment, Sarah. Let's get started."

"Now?"

"Why not? Are you busy tonight?"

"I . . . I was just on my way out."

"Do you have another appointment?"

Sarah consulted the daily planner next to her phone on the corner of her desk. She knew perfectly well she was free for the evening, but she needed a second to collect her muddled thoughts. "No, I don't have an—"

"Terrific." Richard stood and pulled Sarah's coat from a hook behind the door. "We can talk over dinner. Let's go."

Sarah felt somehow that she had lost control of the situation, but before she could think Richard was already helping her into her coat.

"At least let me grab my purse," Sarah said, still struggling to make sense out of his sudden reappearance into her life.

"Dinner really isn't necessary," she protested a few minutes later, after she had locked the building and he was escorting her along the sidewalk.

He stopped and turned to face her. "Have you eaten?"

"No."

"Then dinner is necessary. I don't want you to skip meals on my account." He swung open the door of his car, which was parked at the curb.

Sarah remained silent as they drove through Middletown, pondering his motivation for his seemingly impulsive decision. When he pulled onto the interstate, her thoughts turned elsewhere.

"Where are you taking me?"

Richard changed lanes and passed a truck before answering. "To dinner. I thought we'd already discussed that."

"I know, but there are dozens of restaurants in Middletown. It isn't necessary—"

"Oh, but it is necessary," he interrupted. "I'm taking you to a Greek restaurant, and there aren't any in Middletown."

"You mean we're going to downtown Detroit?"

"That's right, to the best place in the city. Have you ever eaten at Acropolis?"

"No. I've never been to Greek Town."

A strong hand closed over hers, and squeezed companionably. "That's what I thought. Well, you're in for a treat. Just sit tight and relax for a few minutes. We're almost there."

Sarah sat tight, tighter than an overwound clock. And her heart was ticking—ticking with a beat so strong she imagined Richard could hear it in the quiet interior of the car. She'd suspected the first time she'd seen him that he was a threat to her orderly, uncomplicated life. Now she *knew* he was. He could turn her life inside out—if she let him.

When he withdrew his hand, she felt her breath threatening to leave her. Darned if she hadn't missed his touch, his voice, his boyish grin.

By the time they reached their destination, Sarah was on the verge of becoming giddy. She was even more nervous, if that were humanly possible, than she'd been on the night of their first dinner together. She hoped that her legs would support her as they walked the short distance from the parking garage across the street to The Acropolis.

An attractive middle-aged man with a full head of dark hair greeted Richard by name as they entered the dimly lit restaurant. "I have a quiet, private table waiting for you, Dr. Collier." He led them around several tables, through a stone archway, to a secluded area bathed in soft candlelight from flickering wall sconces. He handed each of them a menu. "Sophia will be right with you," he said before leaving.

Sarah tried to open the thin parchment pages but her hands were shaking so rapidly the menu fluttered like a Japanese fan.

"Are you familiar with Greek food?" Richard asked, scanning the pages, obviously having no difficulty with his menu.

Sarah shook her head.

"They have some American selections, but if you're feeling adventurous, I'd recommend trying something Greek."

Before Sarah could answer, a woman wearing a bright red tunic over a long black skirt approached their table.

"Sophia!" Richard called. "How's that new grandson?"

Sophia smiled. "He's nearly fifteen pounds and not even three months old. Ah, he'll be a big boy, like my Nicholas. No babies for you yet, Dr. Collier?" She shook her finger in disapproval. "What a shame." She looked across at Sarah but gestured to Richard. "This one, he loves the babies. He'll make a good papa."

Sarah reached for her water goblet and gulped down several mouthfuls. Sophia was still staring and smiling at Sarah when she put the empty glass back onto the table.

"What's your speciality tonight?" Richard asked finally, after Sarah thought she could not endure the woman's narrow-eyed scrutiny a second longer.

Sophia pulled a pencil from behind her left ear and began writing on a pad. "You'll want to start with the Saganaki. That's flaming cheese," she explained. "Next, salad, of course, then either the grilled lamb or chicken Kapama."

"Why don't you bring us one of each?" Richard suggested. "Do you have moussaka tonight?"

"We always have moussaka! Now, I'll bring you some ouzo. You'll love it," she told Sarah. "It's brandy that tastes like licorice."

Sarah nodded politely, but she had every intention of staying completely away from alcohol. Her head was already spinning.

"How did you meet Sophia?" Sarah ventured after the woman had walked away.

"The entire Andronico clan are my patients," Richard told her. "Sophia and Nick have eleven children. They're all very interesting. Their oldest son plays professional football. One of their daughters is a harpist for the symphony."

"It sounds like you know them very well."

Richard nodded. "Sophia was one of my first patients. I know there are lots of dentists closer to where she lives, but for nearly seven years she has kept coming back to Middletown, and bringing her kids. And," he continued, propping his elbows onto the table, "I enjoy coming down here. It's like another world. Remote, exotic, different. This is where I come when I want to get away from it all."

Sophia returned with a platter of what could only be flaming cheese. The pungent aroma of melting cheese made Sarah's mouth water. She suddenly realized she hadn't taken time for lunch. Perhaps that could account for her light-headedness. She glanced up at Richard's twinkling blue eyes and sincerely doubted that her hunger had anything to do with her state of mind.

Sophia poured a thick brandy from a flask into a pair of glasses before hastening back toward the kitchen.

Sarah was still trying to make sense of the unexpected turn of events that brought her to Greek Town, when her hand brushed Richard's as they both reached for the serving spoon at the same time. It was a casual touch, but it made Sarah feel like this was much more than a business dinner. Or maybe, it was the way he kept looking at her. He was attentive, to say the least.

She had to admit he'd been perfectly charming since he'd picked her up and . . . wait a minute. Her mind backpedaled. Hadn't the owner told Richard he had a table *waiting* for him?

She stared at him through narrowed lids. "How did you know I'd be available for dinner?"

Richard took a sip of ouzo before answering. "I went to your house first. When you didn't answer the door, I decided you were probably still at work."

"You're lucky you caught me," Sarah replied.

"I know," Richard returned with another grin.

The low masculine rumble of his voice coupled with his sensuous smile caused her to feel suddenly parched. She sipped Spartanly at her brandy. It was very rich and sweet, but it burned her throat as she swallowed. Too late, she realized she'd sipped too much. A coughing spasm overcame her, strong enough to bring tears to her eyes.

She regained her dignity with effort, straightened her shoulders, and tried to assume a businesslike posture. "Richard, we should talk about the real reason we're here."

"Right. Do I need to sign some papers or something?"

"No, not yet. But I do have to ask you some questions."

"Ask away, but first have another piece of cheese."

Sarah did. Several pieces in fact, and a salad as well. By the time she realized she was enjoying herself more than she'd intended, Sophia had brought their entrees.

"Here you go," she said, lowering two heaping platters onto the table. "This one is the chicken Kapama. The sauce is a blend of oregano, cloves, allspice, cinnamon, and chilies,'' she told them proudly. ''And this, of course, is the lamb and your moussaka.''

''It all looks wonderful,'' Richard said.

Sophia smiled. ''I'll come back when you're ready for dessert.''

A half hour later Sarah wasn't certain if she had any room for dessert, but when Sophia enthusiastically described the Loukoumathes, a puffy yeast doughnut covered with honey and chopped pecans, Sarah agreed to try some.

It wasn't until they were drinking their after-dinner coffee that Sarah broached the subject that had been ping-ponging through her mind all evening.

''How much thought have you really given to buying a home?''

Richard reached across the small table and caught her hands as she twisted the linen napkin lying next to her empty coffee cup. ''Quite a bit. Why?''

Sarah swallowed and tried to convince herself there was nothing to be nervous about. He was just another client. She was a capable real estate salesperson. She cleared her throat before speaking. ''Buying a home is one of the most important decisions a person can make.''

''Yes, I'm aware of that.''

''Are you prepared to make the necessary legal and financial commitments?''

Richard turned his head quizzically. ''Do you drill all of your customers like this?''

"All of my first-time buyers, yes."

Richard tugged on the knot of his tie. "Are you going to make me promise that when I buy a house I'll clean it and mow the lawn and plant flowers, too?"

"What you do with the property after you purchase it is strictly your business. It is my business, however, to make certain you're a bona fide, qualified, serious buyer."

"I am."

"Okay, then let's establish some priorities." She pulled a notebook from her purse and opened it on the table. "I'd like to make a list of the features of your ideal home. Then we can discuss what you would forego if you need to scale back."

Richard took another drink of coffee and settled back onto his chair. "Okay, let's do it."

Sarah moistened her lips. "Would you prefer to have a custom built home or to move into an existing one?"

"I guess I'd prefer an older house, but one that has been well maintained."

"How large?"

"Three to four thousand square feet should do."

"That's a lot of house for one person."

"You're right, Sarah, it is."

Sarah cleared her throat. "How many bedrooms?"

"At least four, and I'd like a main floor den, if that's possible."

"Number of bathrooms?"

"I haven't really given that a lot of thought. Can I let you know later on that one?"

Sarah nodded. "I'll leave that part blank. Would you prefer a galley or country-style kitchen?"

"Big with lots of cupboards. And a pantry. A walk-in pantry."

"Fireplace?"

"Definitely. And some skylights too. I like lots of natural light."

"That may be difficult to find in an older house, but I'll make a note of it."

Sarah kept writing and focused her eyes on her pen when she asked, "What price range?"

"I'm assuming we'll be looking in the older section of town on the east side? Possibly in Brookway Heights?" Richard asked.

Sarah glanced up at him. So, he had done his homework. He knew exactly where the choice homes were located. But did he have any idea of how much they were worth? She shifted uncomfortably. Now what? Should she ask him how much money he made? She had to have some idea of the amount he intended to spend, and there was no tiptoeing around the issue. Now was as good of time as any to find out.

"Most of the homes in that area are in the three- to six-hundred-thousand-dollar price range."

Richard nodded without flinching.

Sarah, however, was trembling clear down to her shoes. "Before we go out and seriously look at homes,

I'll call some lenders and find out exact mortgage rates,'' she said, struggling to keep her voice steady. *Come on*, a little whisper inside urged. *Explain the loan procedure. You've done it a hundred times.*

"Loan terms will help determine how much you'll be able to afford. There are several lending institutions, and the rates fluctuate.'' She simply couldn't go on. She knew she was beginning to sound like the coaching tape she'd made for new agents.

Richard smiled at her. "I'm confident you'll be able to help me find a home in a neighborhood that will maintain its value. The price isn't really an issue with me.''

"It isn't?''

Richard shook his head. "Borrowing money won't be a problem, Sarah.''

"It won't?'' She could have swallowed her tongue as her voice squeaked.

"I'll see to it that you get a copy of my investment portfolio. You can feel free to go over it.''

Mutely, she stared at him. She'd reviewed financial statements to qualify buyers hundreds of times. It was part of her job. And yet with Richard, somehow it was going to seem like an invasion of his privacy.

"When we go house hunting, what kinds of things will you be looking for?'' he wanted to know.

"Me?''

"Sure, we'll be working as a team. I want your input on everything.''

"The final decision will be yours, Richard. After all, you're the person who'll be living in the house."

For some strange reason, Richard only grinned.

Back at her office, Richard parked his car and walked with Sarah to her Bronco. All she had to do was to thank him for dinner and arrange for a time to begin house hunting. Yet, with each step she took, she felt a stronger and stronger reluctance to leave him.

"When can I see you again?" he asked as she inserted her key into the lock.

Slightly baffled by his question, Sarah turned to face him. "See me again?" she repeated hesitantly.

"To look at houses," he clarified. "Won't we be going out together soon?"

Sarah nodded. Of course they would. Where was her mind? "Tomorrow's Saturday. Will you be available in the afternoon?"

"For you Sarah, I'm available all day." The sincerity in his eyes and in his tone made her heart somersault. A smile crinkled the corners of his mustache. "I could come at noon, and we could go out for lunch," he suggested.

Again, all Sarah could do was nod.

He bent his head and brushed a kiss against her lips. The touch was gone before she could respond. And so was he. He'd helped her into the Bronco, closed the door, and walked away.

And he'd kissed her.

How long she sat numbly behind the steering wheel, she didn't know. What she did know was that another car had pulled next to hers. A quick glimpse told her it was Richard. They lowered their windows at the same time.

"Is something wrong with your car?" he asked.

"No . . . I haven't turned it on yet," Sarah responded, feeling more than foolish.

"It's pretty cold tonight. I'll wait here to make sure you don't have fuel-line freeze-up," he offered.

Sarah turned the key and, thankfully, the engine started immediately. "I'll see you at noon in my office," she called, keeping her eyes focused on her instrument panel. She pulled away and had driven several blocks before she realized she'd forgotten to raise her window.

She had to get a grip on herself before it was too late. But too late for what? she asked herself. She'd already fallen in love with Richard Collier. And now, at least for the next several weeks, she'd be seeing him constantly. The thought made her heart pound like a sledgehammer.

Chapter 9

The following morning flashed by Sarah in a blur. People came and went. Phone calls were answered and returned. Questions were asked and decisions made. Now, at quarter to twelve, as she sat alone in her office, Sarah's mind was singularly focused. On Richard.

Stacked in front of her were several information sheets detailing features of a dozen homes. Would any of them interest him? Would he still want to go house hunting even though eight inches of new snow had fallen during the night? Would a temperature including the wind-chill factor of minus five degrees deter him? If he were a serious buyer, the weather wouldn't stop him. But that was the whole point, wasn't it?

She couldn't help wondering if indeed he was as truly committed as he professed to be. And if he was, would he find a house today or would it become a drawn-out process, taking up her time for several months?

Preoccupied in her thoughts, Sarah nearly jumped out of her skin at the sound of a loud knock on her door.

"Yes?" she asked, a breathless catch to her voice.

The door swung open and Richard entered her office. Suddenly, the tingling thrill of anticipation she had felt all morning intensified, as did the knot of excitement in the pit of her stomach.

He greeted her with a warm, "Hello!" His smile was wide. His eyes were twinkling. "Evelyn was on the phone, so she motioned for me to come on back. I hope I'm not interrupting anything."

"Not at all. I'm ready for you," Sarah told him, pleading with herself to keep her voice steady. "Please have a seat."

Richard shrugged off his bright blue ski jacket, hung it behind the door, then sat in the chair across the desk from Sarah. He gestured to the papers in front of her. "Are those some of the houses we're going to look at?"

"If they interest you, yes. Let's go over each of them, and if you'd like to see any, I'll call the listing agent and arrange for a viewing time." She slid an information sheet over to him. "This one has been on the market since last October," Sarah explained while Richard glanced at the picture. "It's in a good neighborhood and has the right number of square feet, but the plumbing needs work. That's typical of quite a few older homes."

After they discussed the pros and cons of each selection, Richard enthusiastically proclaimed that he wanted to see them all.

"All right, I'll need to use the phone for a few minutes. If you like, Evelyn can make a cup of coffee for you while you wait."

Richard nodded and left Sarah to do her calling. He returned ten minutes later with two steaming cups. Sarah smelled the sweet aroma of chocolate before he handed one to her.

"I'm assuming that since you always order something chocolate from a dessert menu, you like this stuff."

Sarah rewarded him with a smile. "You're very observant, Dr. Collier. Chocolate is one of my weaknesses."

"What are your others?" he asked, casually propping against her desk.

She could feel an unwelcome blush creep onto her cheeks. "Cuddly, stuffed animals," she replied while dialing another agent. She hoped the answer would satisfy him, but judging from the way he kept smiling and nodding, she doubted that it would.

Despite Richard's unnerving presence, Sarah managed to finish making the calls. She swallowed the last sip of her cocoa and glanced at her watch. "I'd like to show you seven homes this afternoon," she told him. He was now examining the pictures on her wall as if they interested him. "We should have time to see them all after lunch, which, incidentally, will be my treat." She stood and opened her desk drawer.

"Wait," he said as she pulled her car keys from a

wooden tray. "The roads are still treacherous. Why don't you leave your car here, and I'll bring you back later?"

"I'm more than used to driving on snow and besides, I'm familiar with all the locations," she protested.

"Then you can direct me," he countered, while helping her into her coat. Sarah knew from experience that Richard, like her mother, seldom took no for an answer.

When they walked outside, the glaring brightness reflected from the snow caused Sarah to squint. Sunglasses would be helpful, but she didn't want to take time to go back into the building for them. Instead, she shielded her eyes with her hands and scanned the crowded parking lot for Richard's silver BMW.

He stopped abruptly, nearly causing her to run into him, and gently patted the hood of a vintage Mustang. The car had been beautifully reconditioned, its custom paint job, a bright cherry red, gleaming with hand-rubbed gloss.

"Is this yours?" she asked, surprised and yet not.

He nodded proudly. "It's the first car I ever owned. I bought it for myself too." His gaze flickered to the Mustang, then back to Sarah. "When I find something I like, I keep it. Here, let me help you inside," he said as he unlocked and opened the door.

After taking his place behind the wheel, he started the engine and turned the heater to high. "I installed the seatbelts myself," he told Sarah, buckling his.

"These earlier models didn't come equipped with many safety features."

Sarah looked around the interior of the car, taking in the bright white leather seats and polished chrome. "It's certainly in immaculate condition," she commented.

"Thanks. I did a lot of work on it last summer. I even put in a new engine." He downshifted and asked, "Have you ever driven a four speed?"

Sarah laughed. "I'm afraid not. I'm not very mechanical, and automatics seem so much easier to control."

"Ah, but you can't get a real feel for the road, driving an automatic. When the snow melts I'll teach you how to drive a stick. You'll love it."

Sarah watched as he depressed the clutch with his left foot then shifted into first one gear then another with his right hand, all the while steering with the other. "I don't think I would ever remember what I was supposed to do. It looks pretty complicated."

"There's nothing to it," Richard returned. Quite unexpectedly he reached for Sarah's hand and placed it on the smooth, wooded gearshift-knob. "We're in third now, and after I accelerate to about forty, we'll pull it down into fourth, like this."

Her whole arm quivered from the contact. "Don't worry," he told her. "I've got everything under control."

But *she* didn't. She'd lost control and the realization

frightened her. Sarah withdrew her hand. "We're coming close to the restaurant. I'd better start paying attention to the streets," she said. *And paying less attention to you*, she told herself sternly.

After having a soup and salad bar lunch, they were back in the car, heading toward the first house on Sarah's list.

"This is the Historic District," she explained. "The homes are generally well maintained but need updating to more modern standards. At the next stop sign, turn left. The house we're looking for will be the fourth one on the right."

"We're in luck. The walk has been cleared," Richard said as he brought the car to a halt.

Sarah looked down at her slush-coated boots that rested on his sparkling clean floormats. Maybe she should have brought some paper towels. Maybe she should have driven. Maybe she should pull herself together and get out of the car. This was business, she had to remind herself, not a date to the prom.

Richard supported her elbow as they climbed a pair of steps leading to a wide, brick sidewalk. "This house is a Dutch Colonial," Sarah said, struggling to slip back into her realtor mode.

"It looks like a typical two-story to me." Richard stopped midway up the walk to study the design of the house. "What makes it a Dutch Colonial?" he asked after a few seconds.

"The gambrel roof, for one thing, and eaves that

flare outward. It also has a Dutch-style front door and small paned windows.''

Richard nodded.

''Now, across the street is a New England Colonial,'' Sarah explained.

Richard turned around to look.

''See the difference? It has white clapboards with dark green wooden shutters and chimneys at both ends.''

''I'll be darned. They really are different once you take a good look at them. I'm impressed. You really know your houses.''

''It's all part of my business,'' Sarah said with a small smile. She approached the front door, rang the bell, then reached for a gold metal box hanging through the handle. ''The listing agent told me that the owner prefers not to be home when the house is being shown, so in all probability, he isn't here,'' she said while turning a combination dial. ''This is a lock box, and there's a key inside.'' She promptly and efficiently removed the key and opened the door.

While inside, Richard said very little, only commenting on the purple-and orange-striped wallpaper in an upstairs bedroom. They were in and out in less than five minutes. The house was not only a decorator's nightmare but musty and drafty as well.

On the way to the second house, Richard stopped in front of an English Tudor. ''That's an impressive place. Too bad it isn't for sale. It looks great from out here.''

''That's called 'curb appeal,' and you're right, it's lovely. Would you like to go through a few Tudors?''

''Does that style appeal to you?''

''You're the client, Richard. My preferences aren't important.''

He reached for her hand and squeezed it. ''Your preferences *are* important, Sarah. I value your opinions. You've had a lot more experience than I have at this type of thing. If you see a house you especially like, I want you to tell me.''

Richard's request stunned her. He'd impressed her as a man who knew what he wanted. Why would he want *her* to choose his house? It simply didn't make any sense. Sarah noticed a muscle twitching in his cheek. Could he be nervous? she wondered. He turned to her and smiled. His eyes had a fascinating glow. When his gaze captured hers, Sarah felt a familiar blush creeping on to her cheeks.

Sitting elbow-to-elbow next to him in the compact car made her edgy, to say the least. She still hadn't been able to shake a sense of danger that had nothing to do with the slippery streets.

They looked at a half-dozen more houses that afternoon. Richard had insisted on Sarah giving him her opinion on each of them. None really impressed her, and she told him so. Her policy of complete honesty had lost her a few sales in the past, but she'd rather live with less profit than have a dissatisfied customer.

By the time they returned to the real estate office, everyone else had gone home. It was after six o'clock, and Sarah felt exhausted.

Richard obviously sensed her fatigue. "Does work usually wear you out like this?" he asked as he took the key from her hand and unlocked the door. She noticed that his eyes held genuine concern when she glanced up to thank him for holding the door open for her to enter the lobby.

"My job isn't always this hectic. Since I was gone last weekend, I still have some catching up to do."

"And I've caused you to work late two days in a row," Richard said softly.

Sarah laughed. "Sometimes I spend an entire week with a client." She patted the sleeve of his jacket. "But don't worry, we won't always need to spend this much time together. In the beginning, I like to get a good idea of what my customers are looking for. Now that I know what you hope to find, I'll be more selective in setting up appointments."

When they came to her office, she opened the door, flipped on the light, and took off her coat.

Richard followed her into the room. "You're pretty remarkable, do you know that?" he asked.

"I'm just doing my job," she said. She sat down at her desk and immediately turned on her computer monitor.

He shook his head. "You have a real knack for what you do. A talent. You seemed to sense that I didn't feel right about a house before I even opened my mouth. How did you figure it out?"

"I can always tell whether or not my clients are interested in a property by the speed with which they walk through the house."

"Oh?"

Without looking up at him, she continued, "Uh huh. The slower people walk, the more interested they are. You practically raced through every one of them." She busied herself at the computer terminal, bringing up the file of the day's action.

Richard took a seat and seemed to contemplate her words. "Maybe I was just anxious," he said after a few minutes.

Sarah nodded. "You were anxious, all right. Anxious to leave." She continued to stare at the computer screen. "If you'd like to make yourself comfortable for a few minutes, I'll make you a list of homes that sold recently in neighborhoods like the ones you're interested in. We can do a cost-per-square-foot analysis. Would you like a cup of coffee?"

"Not here, but we could go out for one."

Sarah glanced up at him. He looked so beguiling. And his offer was so tempting . . . and so dangerous to her emotional well-being, she reminded herself quickly. "I've got a lot of housework waiting for me, and since I have an open house scheduled for tomorrow, I'd better stay home tonight.''

His brows rose and his expression was one of disbelief. ''You're actually going to clean your house after putting in a day like you did?''

Sarah shrugged. ''I do what I have to do.''

''Why don't you hire a cleaning service?'' Richard asked.

''My house isn't that large,'' Sarah countered.

''Neither is my apartment, but I have someone come in once a week. I can give you her name and—''

Sarah shook her head. ''I'd rather clean my own house.''

''Ah,'' Richard responded with a nod. ''I'd forgotten how independent you are.'' He pushed himself to his feet and slowly walked to the door. ''Since you're so busy, I'll be going. I think on my way home I'll stop for a nice, quiet dinner. Then after I eat I'll go by the video store and rent two or three old movies, go home and make some popcorn, and build a rip-roaring fire.'' He stepped into the hallway and called to Sarah. ''Too bad you won't be able to join me.''

Too bad indeed, Sarah thought. She knew perfectly well that sharing a cozy evening with Richard would be more taxing on her than cleaning out her attic, basement, and garage. ''I'll call you when I find some more houses.''

''Good. I'll leave my answering machine on so I

won't miss your call. I'll be gone most of the day tomorrow.''

Where? Sarah wondered, then immediately chastised herself. She had no business knowing. Yet she could speculate. An eligible bachelor like Richard probably had a date.

''I don't have a date,'' Richard informed her, as if he had read her thoughts, causing her cheeks to flame scarlet. ''Mom usually makes dinner for me on Sundays, then Dad and I watch football or basketball on TV.''

''Oh,'' she murmured. ''Have a nice time.''

''I intend to,'' he said, then left.

Later that evening, after dusting and vacuuming her entire house, Sarah sat down at the kitchen table and glanced at the mail while she waited for the microwave to cook her frozen dinner. There wasn't much of interest, just a phone bill, coupons for a new dry cleaner, and . . . a postcard from her mother.

She stared at the colorful picture of the Eiffel Tower. No doubt her mother was in the midst of some madcap adventure in Paris. She must have mailed the card the same day she'd arrived, Sarah thought, judging by the speed at which she'd received it. How much trouble could her mother have gotten into in that short amount of time?

Sarah's curiosity finally got the better of her, and she flipped the card over.

Andora's unmistakable flowing script brought a slight smile to Sarah's face. Her mother's handwriting was as unique as her personality.

Bonjour Dear Daughter,
Paris is delightful. Very romantic. Today was cold and rainy but the weather didn't dampen my spirits. I've been shopping, dining and dancing. I won't be coming home until Tuesday now. I'll visit then and tell you all the wonderful details of my trip.
Au Revoir,
Mother

When she finished reading, Sarah put the postcard on the table and simply sat there for a few minutes, chin in cupped hands. A shopping trip, her mother had called it. A chance to buy some new spring clothes. Now she was dancing.

It made Sarah's evening seem dull. But, she finally admitted to herself, even Paris didn't sound as good as old movies, popcorn, a roaring fire . . . and Richard.

Chapter 10

"Well?" Evelyn prompted the next day, before Sarah had taken off her coat. "Did you have any luck finding a house for Dr. Collier?"

"Not yet, but I'm still looking," Sarah returned with as much nonchalance as she could muster. She tugged off her gloves and rifled through the heaping stack of mail and messages piled into her "in" box.

"Will you get to see him again today?" Evelyn asked, obviously not willing to let the matter rest.

Sarah shrugged. "Not unless something new comes onto the market."

Evelyn clapped her hands then rubbed them together. "Just think, you'll have the perfect excuse to call him, and spend the day with him, and—"

"Please," Sarah interrupted, glancing around anxiously for signs of other agents. To her relief, she didn't see anyone. "I don't want you to get the wrong impression of my relationship with Dr. Collier. He simply wants me to help him purchase a house."

"And he *simply* went with you to the Caribbean," Evelyn reminded her.

Sarah rolled her eyes. "I had absolutely nothing to do with those plans."

"Oh? You two just happened to meet on a beach in paradise?"

"Something like that," Sarah said noncommittally. She gnawed her bottom lip. There was something she was dying to know, but wasn't sure how to ask without increasing speculation. *Just blurt it out*, a little voice inside urged. Since she couldn't think of another way to broach the subject, she did just that.

"By the way, Evelyn, how do you and Bradley know Richard?"

Evelyn beamed. "So you're interested, huh?"

"Just curious," Sarah ventured.

"He's our dentist," Bradley's wife replied. "One of the ladies in my bridge club recommended him to us years ago. His motto is 'I cater to cowards'. And he does. He's the most gentle dentist I've ever gone to. I actually relax and listen to classical music while he's working on my teeth. He's just a wonderful man, don't you think so?"

Sarah carefully kept her expression in check. "I'm sure he's nice."

Evelyn chuckled. "Honey, if 'nice' is the only word you can come up with to describe Richard Collier, then maybe you should see an eye doctor. There must be dozens of his patients who'd—pardon the pun—give their eyeteeth for a date with that sexy dentist."

Sarah merely nodded and absently opened an envelope.

"It's not just the fact that he's wealthy, though you wouldn't know it to speak with him. He's not the uppity type, if you know what I mean," Evelyn went on, "but he's so handsome. And you spent an entire weekend with him and only noticed he's *nice*?"

Sarah decided it was time to change the subject. "Did Mrs. McCoy call this morning?"

Evelyn looked irritated. "Yes, I took a message for you. She'll be expecting you at two o'clock."

"Perfect. That will still give me time to check on a vacant property I'm watching on Lincoln Street." Not waiting for another round of praise about Richard from her receptionist, Sarah pulled on her gloves and left.

When Sarah walked back into Middletown Realty late that afternoon, the office was abuzz with working agents. The moment she was noticed, however, the noise level diminished, and she was greeted with several curious stares and even more ear-to-ear grins. She wondered why until she opened the door to her private office.

There, seated in the chair behind her desk, was the most gigantic stuffed panda bear she'd ever seen. A big blue bow adorned its neck and its arms were outstretched as if offering her a hug.

"Can you guess who brought it?" Evelyn asked from the hallway.

Sarah sighed. She already knew. "Probably a practical joker," she answered in an attempt to minimize the attention she was getting. Her effort was in vain.

"I saw who it was," another agent said, breezing into Sarah's office. "He was tall, and blond, and handsome. He had a mustache too, and the bluest eyes."

"Wasn't he the same man who was in here yesterday asking for Sarah around lunch time?" someone else added, as she joined the group.

"He most certainly was," Evelyn confirmed. "Dr. Richard Collier. Will you be seeing him again tonight?"

"The dentist! I heard he's a very eligible bachelor. Are you dating him?" the first woman wanted to know.

"It must be weird dating a dentist," the second one commented. "Does he stare at your teeth all the time you're with him?"

Sarah threw her arms into the air. "No, no, and no!" She took another look at the smiling animal that occupied her chair, then added, "I can't imagine what possessed him to buy me *that*."

"I think it's sweet of him."

"I think he's sweet on you."

A ripple of laughter coursed through the room as three more agents squeezed into the now crowded office. Sarah closed her eyes and groaned.

"What's all the commotion about?" a male voice asked. Sarah opened her eyes to find Bradley craning his neck from the doorway. When the group parted to give him a view, he scratched his head in an obvious state of befuddlement. "Who's the visitor?"

"It's a gift from an admirer," Evelyn supplied.

"It's a gift from a client," Sarah corrected.

"Richard Collier?" Bradley guessed.

Sarah nodded.

"Interesting," Bradley said, nodding his head. "I ran into Dr. Collier in the parking lot early this afternoon. I was leaving and he was arriving. Now that I think of it, he did open his trunk just as I walked away. I'll be darned. A panda."

"Yes, a panda." She caught the grins on the faces of two men standing in the hallway. Annoyed, she said, "If you'll all excuse me, I have several phone calls to return." With that she promptly picked up her panda and deposited him in another chair.

Everyone left except Bradley. He moseyed over to the window, lifted the blinds, and peered into the parking lot before sitting in the armchair beside Sarah's desk.

She swiveled her chair around to face him. "Something on your mind?"

"Not 'something', someone. You. Richard and I had a nice little chat about you."

"Richard talked to you about *me*?"

Bradley smiled and nodded. "He thinks you work too hard."

"I didn't realize my work habits were his concern."

The older man stared at the ceiling before his eyes

met Sarah's with a leveling gaze. "Apparently they are. And I happen to agree with him."

"Now, Bradley—"

Her partner held up his hands. "No, Sarah, hear me out. Today I took the liberty of interviewing another agent. If we can get three or four more people in here, then you and I can both enjoy some time off."

"You may be ready to retire, Bradley, but I'm not. I enjoy putting in long hours."

"That may change."

Instantly, Sarah bristled. "What do you mean by that?"

"You're a young woman, Sarah. Someday you'll meet someone and want to spend more time with him and less time in here. We've got to plan for the future."

"I don't anticipate getting married anytime soon."

"But when you do, we want to protect our investment."

Sarah could tell by the worry lines across her partner's brow that he honestly thought she might someday shirk her responsibilities. "This business is my top priority," she assured him. The workload was overwhelming, but she didn't want Bradley to feel pressured into doing more than he should. "Would you like to advertise for additional agents?"

Bradley nodded enthusiastically. "That's the spirit," he said as he stood. "I'm ready to close up shop. How about you?"

"I guess I can make my calls from home." Sarah rose, walked to the door and stuck her head out.

Bradley laughed. "I think everyone's gone except my devoted wife. The coast is probably clear to make an exit with your furry friend."

"That's not funny," Sarah said.

Bradley responded with a wink.

That evening Sarah was sure that Richard would call. She and the panda had sat side by side watching an old Clark Gable movie. Sarah made popcorn. The panda held the bowl. By the time the late news broadcast was over and Richard still hadn't called, she got ready for bed. She curled in a tight ball beneath the quilt and told herself she had no reason to feel disappointed. After all, she could have called and thanked him for the gift. But did she really want to encourage him?

Tonight was one of the few times she regretted her solitary lifestyle. If there had been someone to share her lonely moments, some friend she could talk to, perhaps she wouldn't feel so empty and cold.

Anonymity had been her goal all of her life. As she matured, the fewer friends she made. She always rationalized that since she moved so frequently, she'd never live in any one place long enough to cultivate a lasting friendship. As time went by, even in college, the other students had given up trying to get to know her. Except David.

Now there was no one she could call.

* * *

The following week passed without a word from Richard. Nosy questions from the office gossips had sparked a flicker of annoyance in Sarah on Monday. When she received an arrangement of sweetheart roses without an acknowledgment card on Wednesday, fuel was added to the fire. Glances were exchanged and eyebrows were raised whenever she walked into a room.

It seemed no one had anything better to talk about than the mysterious absence of Dr. Collier. Everything was speculated and discussed at length from the possibility of a lovers' quarrel to another woman taking Sarah's place. By Saturday morning Sarah thought she would scream if one more person mentioned Richard's name.

When a new client phoned and asked if she had time to show him and his wife several homes, Sarah jumped at the chance.

Her elation, however, was short lived. Perhaps it was because she was less tolerant than usual, but within the first ten minutes in the company of Mr. and Mrs. Templeton, she knew they would never rank among her favorite clients. Every other comment from Margaret Templeton was "This isn't at all what we're used to" or "In Texas the quality is far superior to this." With that kind of attitude, Sarah could predict that the woman would be utterly miserable during her stay in Michigan.

Trying hard to ignore the woman's negativity, Sarah showed the couple three houses, treated them to lunch, then tromped through the snow to let them inspect a building site in a subdivision scheduled for construction in the spring. Mr. Templeton had said very little, but his wife had found one fault after another. In one embarrassing instance the woman had actually called a window treatment cheap in comparison to her own back home, voicing her criticism within earshot of the present owner.

By the time Sarah had driven them back to their hotel, which was inconveniently located on the other side of Detroit, her strongest desire was never to see them again. She couldn't remember ever disliking clients as much. Glancing at her watch, she discovered it was only two-thirty. The thought of returning to the office had her stomach churning. On the spur of the moment, she decided to play hooky.

It took almost forty-five minutes to get back to Middletown and another two hours to run an assortment of errands. Even after that length of time, she was still fuming as she juggled a bag of groceries and her dry cleaning while she tried to unlock the back door. Her next house would have an attached garage and an automatic opener, she vowed.

The phone was ringing when she entered, and she almost decided to let her answering machine pick up the call. But the incessant ringing got on her already frazzled nerves, so she set her bundles down on the kitchen table and answered it.

''You sound out of breath,'' a familiar baritone voice said.

''I just came in. What can I do for you, Richard?'' Sarah was proud of her calm, businesslike tone.

''It's been a few days since I've heard from you,'' he said. ''I was beginning to wonder if you still wanted to work with me.''

''Of course I do.'' Sarah swallowed before continuing. ''Nothing new has come onto the market.''

There was a long pause, and then he said, ''Actually, that wasn't why I called you.''

''It wasn't?''

She heard him clear his throat before speaking again. ''Today is my partner and his wife's tenth wedding anniversary, and their baby-sitter caught that flu that's going around. They tried to get someone else, but tonight is the high school Valentine's Dance, and well . . . I was hoping you weren't busy.''

''Are you asking *me* to baby-sit?'' Sarah asked, scarcely believing his question.

Richard chuckled. ''Do you have other plans?''

Sarah felt trapped. ''Well . . . '' she stalled. She mulled the idea over in her mind, not wanting to commit herself immediately.

She must have hesitated too long because Richard added, ''Jack and Marlene are really in a bind. They have tickets to a concert in Detroit at the Renaissance Center.''

His voice sounded so sincere, and since she had nothing better to do than eat a chicken pot pie from the freezer and finish a book she'd started a month ago, Sarah guessed it would be all right to offer her assistance. ''Okay, I'll do it.''

''Great! The concert doesn't start until nine, but they want to go out to dinner first. How about if I come for you at six-thirty?''

Sarah sighed. ''There's not a trace of snow on the streets tonight. If you'll give me directions, I can drive myself.''

''Uh, Sarah?''

''Yes, Richard.''

''Didn't I mention that we'll be watching the kids together?''

''No, you didn't.''

''I'd do it myself except I don't have much experience changing diapers. Little Jeremy is four and won't be too much of a problem, but Cassandra is only seven months, and, well, I thought we could help each other.''

Sarah remained silent for several seconds, prompting Richard to ask, ''Are you still there?''

''I'm here.'' *And here is where I'd rather stay*, she added to herself.

''Don't eat before I pick you up. We can order out for a pizza after the kids are asleep.''

Sarah sighed again. "All right."

"Sarah?"

"Yes?"

"Thanks."

"You'd better wait to thank me until later. I've never changed a diaper in my life."

Richard's deep laughter was still echoing in her ear when Sarah returned the phone to its cradle and stared at the kitchen wall. Had she actually volunteered to spend an evening baby-sitting? With Richard? She must be out of her mind.

She had a little over an hour to get ready, and she was going to need every second. She swiftly put away her groceries and hung up the plastic-draped garments from the cleaners. Next on her agenda was a hot bath to rid herself of the chill that had penetrated her bones since her trek across a snow-covered field with the Templetons.

Her bath complete and her body wrapped in a soft, thick velour robe, she stood before her open closet. What did one wear to baby-sit? she wondered. Certainly nothing fancy. She settled on cream-colored corduroy slacks and a red turtleneck pullover topped with a red, cream, and black plaid cardigan sweater.

At precisely half past six the bell rang. When she opened the door, the first thing Sarah saw was an enormous bouquet of long-stemmed red roses.

"For you," Richard said, placing them in her hands.

Sarah stood speechless and watched him walk into

her living room and smile at the sight of the panda on her sofa. She'd intended to move him to another room before Richard came.

"I'm glad you decided to give Mr. Panda a home," he said, rubbing the white and black fur. He picked a piece of popcorn from the bear's shoulder and held it up for Sarah's inspection. "Don't tell me you're feeding him people food," he teased.

"Only when he lets me choose the movie," Sarah said, suddenly feeling more lighthearted than she had in days. "Thank you for the flowers, too. As soon as I put them in some water, I'll be ready to go."

"I'll turn on a light for Mr. Panda so he won't have to sit alone in the dark while you're gone."

"You're so thoughtful," Sarah called from the kitchen.

"I try to be," Richard returned.

Moments later, they were heading west to a newly developed suburban community. "Jack and Marlene bought a house last fall," Richard told Sarah. She wondered if his partner's recent purchase had anything to do with Richard's desire to move.

He pulled into the driveway of a sprawling one-story contemporary. Jack met them at the door. He wasn't as tall as Richard but equally trim and fit.

"You must be Sarah," he said, offering her his hand. "Richard's told me all about you. I hope you like kids."

Before Sarah could comment, a small red-haired boy

wearing a footed sleeper ran up to Richard and wrapped his arms around his legs. "Uncle Richard, will you tell me a monster story?"

Richard lifted the boy into his arms. "Do you promise to be good tonight, Jeremy?"

A red head bobbed up and down.

"Okay when it's bedtime, I'll tell you a story."

"With scary monsters," the child reminded him.

Just then, a woman who could only be Jeremy's mother joined them. She smiled as she pried a fistful of her curly auburn hair from the clenched fist of the baby in her arms. "I'm Marlene and this is Cassandra," she told Sarah, placing the infant in her arms. The baby immediately latched onto Sarah's hair.

Richard carefully pulled Cassandra's hand away, and she started to cry.

"Jack, I don't know if this is such a good idea, leaving Richard and Sarah here like this," Marlene said, having to raise her voice over the squalling. "The baby is starting to cut teeth and—"

"And you deserve a night off," her husband told her. "My old buddy is a pro with kids," he said, patting Richard on the back. Smiling at Sarah, he added, "You can probably spend the whole evening with your feet propped up. Richard can handle everything."

Sarah doubted it but didn't voice her thoughts.

"There are bottles in the refrigerator and diapers in the top drawer of the chest in the nursery. I taped a list of emergency numbers to the phone,'' Marlene told them as Jack ushered her to the foyer.

Jack kissed the top of his wife's head as he helped her on with her coat. Marlene glanced up at him with a look that clearly defined the love they felt for one another. Sarah felt a lump forming in the back of her throat. She wondered if they knew just how lucky they were.

With their baby in her arms, she watched them walk hand in hand down the sidewalk to their car. Richard slipped his arm around her shoulder. He was standing so close, she could feel his warm breath on her neck. A shiver coursed through her.

''Do you think it's too early to put the kids to bed?'' Richard whispered in her ear.

''I want some graham crackers,'' Jeremy told them.

Sarah was relieved by his distraction. As long as the kids were awake, she could busy herself and keep her distance from Richard. After they went to sleep . . . that was the part that worried her.

She carefully planned activities that kept the tone light and uncomplicated. For most of the evening Richard played with Jeremy, and she cared for the baby. Once Cassandra had her bottle, she snuggled into Sarah's arms, perfectly contented to be held. Much to Jeremy's delight, Richard told a long story, complete with trolls, giants, and a fire-breathing dragon.

When the time came to put the children to bed, Richard and Jeremy coached Sarah as she changed a diaper. She had to admit it was easier than she'd expected.

True to his word, Richard phoned in an order for a pizza to be delivered, then helped Sarah pick up an assortment of Jeremy's toys from the family room floor. For the next half hour they sat silently at opposite ends of the sofa and watched a popular sitcom. They talked about the weather, rising insurance rates, and car repairs at the kitchen table while they ate their pizza. Much to Sarah's frustration, Richard seemed calm and perfectly at ease while she was a bundle of nerves.

"I really appreciate you coming with me tonight," he said a few minutes later as they stood next to one another at the sink.

Sarah washed a plate and handed it to Richard to dry. "The kids were great," she said. But what happens next? she wondered apprehensively. A few minutes later she found out.

Chapter 11

The dishes finished, Sarah wiped her hands on a towel and said, "I think I'll go check on the kids." She'd taken no more than two steps when Richard gently spun her around to face him. He was smiling. His intriguing blue eyes sought her complete attention, and she didn't want to give it to him. All the conflicting feelings that churned inside her must have shown on her face.

"Relax, Sarah," he whispered.

She went completely numb.

He gently brushed one hand along her cheek and her breathing stopped. When he lowered his head toward her, she ceased to think coherently. He came even nearer. Finally, he was so close it made her dizzy to look at him. She lowered her gaze and waited breathlessly for his lips to meet hers.

He didn't kiss her immediately, as she expected. Instead his lips first sought her cheek before coming to rest gently on her mouth in a tentative, exploring manner as if he were kissing her for the first time. Of their own accord, her arms coiled tightly around his neck, her fingers entwining in his thick, tawny hair, surrendering herself to sensations she'd never before experienced. The rightness of his embrace surprised her.

The awareness that tonight might be the only time she would be held in his arms only served to heighten her emotions to an almost desperate degree.

Finally, she knew she had to pull from his embrace. When she did, Richard looked at her. "What's wrong?"

She gazed at him, mesmerized, trying desperately to summon the words she knew instinctively she should say. But her heart wouldn't let her.

"Sarah, we need to talk."

Her lips were still tingling from his kisses. "I know," she managed to murmur.

He took her hand and led her into the family room. He gestured for her to sit on the sofa and then sat next to her.

"Talk to me," he said softly.

Cautiously she looked at him. Her fingers longed to touch his cheek, his lips. She clutched a pillow in her hands to rid herself of the temptation.

"I have to keep my distance from you," she said, then was horrified that she'd actually voiced the words.

A frown creased his brow. "Why? Am I that threatening?"

"To my sanity, yes," she said truthfully.

"I thought that since we'd spent more time with each other, you'd feel comfortable around me now."

"We haven't exactly been dating," she reminded him.

Richard nodded. "But we have been together."

"Yes."

"Sarah, have you ever wondered why I'm so anxious to buy a house?" he asked.

"It has crossed my mind." *At least a thousand times*, she added to herself.

He shifted his position and leaned back into a corner of the sofa, putting some space between them. He crossed his arms over his chest. "I'm ready for a change in my life. Quite truthfully, I'm envious of the relationship Jack has with Marlene, and I want kids."

Sarah swallowed and tried to digest this information. "Are you planning to marry soon?" she ventured to ask.

"I hope so," Richard told her, then he got up abruptly and went over to the window. "They're back." He looked at his watch. "Can you believe it's almost midnight?"

Sarah scarcely heard him. Her mind was a million miles away. Did Richard already have a special lady in his life? He'd told her he didn't when they were in St. Maarten. Had he found one since? She suspected he had. But where? Did she live in another state? Her head spun with questions she couldn't ask.

After Jack and Marlene thanked them profusely,

Sarah and Richard were on their way. It had started to snow again, and the roads were hazardous. So were Sarah's thoughts, hazardous to her emotional well-being.

Her mind kept turning everything over and always came back to the same conclusion. Regardless of whether Richard had a girlfriend or not, Sarah felt sure his attraction to her was temporary. He was aware of how she felt about lasting relationships. He knew she wasn't marriage material. She'd told him so.

In spite of what he knew, she couldn't deny Richard's strong physical attraction to her. Now she knew where she stood with him. He considered her useful for the time being, but he had other plans for the future. She was just handy. Nothing more.

"You don't need to get out of the car," she said upon arriving home.

Ignoring her, Richard turned off the ignition, got out, and went around to open her door. Sarah beat him to it. She was well on her way up the walk by the time he caught up with her.

"What's your hurry?"

"I'm tired," she replied, for a lack of a better explanation.

The phone was ringing as she opened the door. "Now, who in the world could that be?" she said, negotiating her way around furniture in the darkened living room.

"Hello?"

The nature of the call was something she least expected. After she keenly listened to the details, she hung up the phone and turned to Richard, who was standing at her side.

"That was the police. There's been a break-in at a vacant property I'm watching for a client who's already moved to New York."

"If it's vacant, what could burglars hope to steal?"

"Built-in appliances, garage door openers, security systems, light fixtures—"

"Okay, I get the picture. What do the police want you to do?"

"They asked me to drive over to the house and inspect for damages and make a list of what's missing."

"Drive over!" he repeated, his tone incredulous. "At this hour? Why can't they wait till morning?"

Sarah shrugged. "Police procedure, I guess. An officer will meet me there in ten minutes." She started to walk in the direction of her back door. "Would you mind locking the front door on your way out?" she called to Richard.

"Wait a second!"

Sarah turned around to find him standing directly behind her. "Please, Richard. I don't have a second to wait. It's at least a ten-minute drive and—"

"And I'll be the one doing the driving," Richard finished for her.

"This is my problem, and I can handle it," Sarah said, her voice tight in her chest.

He glared at her. "Right now you're *my* problem, and I'm trying to handle you."

Sarah rolled her eyes. "We're wasting time arguing."

"You're not getting rid of me."

"I really don't want you to come."

"I know," he said as he escorted her back to his car.

When they arrived at the house, several police cars were parked in front. Richard pulled in behind them. Sarah noticed immediately that there were tire tracks in the snow across the yard and that the glass in the front door was broken. She held her breath, fearing the worst.

She soon discovered the house had not only been burglarized but also vandalized. Windows were broken and cupboard doors were ripped off. Everything was cleaned out, even the bathroom mirrors. It took her nearly two hours to file a report, then she had to go over to her office to check the files in order to determine who was the insurance carrier.

By the time Richard took her home, Sarah was physically and emotionally exhausted. And she was shaking.

"I'll make you something hot to drink," he offered, shutting the door behind him.

For the life of her she couldn't figure out why, but

she started to cry. Richard quickly shrugged off his coat then helped Sarah out of hers.

"Why don't you sit down? I'll make a fire. Should I use the wood in the basket?"

Sarah nodded and sat on the floor next to the fireplace. She watched Richard open the grate and pile in some logs. He wadded up some newspaper, stuffed it between the wood, lit a match and tossed it in.

Richard offered her his hand. "Here, let me help you over to the sofa."

As he drew her off the floor and into a standing position, Sarah buried her face in his shoulder. "I'm usually not like this," she sobbed.

"I know," he said, stroking her hair.

She pulled back and looked at him. "I'm glad you were with me. You remembered things I would have forgotten. I've never had to do anything like that before."

"You did just fine, Sarah."

"Richard?"

"Yes?"

"Would you mind staying for just a little while longer? I don't want to be alone right now."

"I'll stay as long as you like."

"Thank you," she whispered, suddenly feeling very sleepy. She stumbled over to the sofa and sat down next to the panda. A log from the fire exploded into a cascade of sparks, and she closed her eyes against the sudden brightness. Sometime later she was only vaguely aware that Richard had sat down beside her.

"Are you still cold?" he murmured.

"Ummm," she responded, only half awake. His breath fluttered the hair at her temple, and she let herself relax even more. Her head fell sideways to rest on his shoulder.

Some part of her knew it was a mistake to be so near to him . . . she should move away . . . but she was so wonderfully warm, his shoulder was so comfortable. And she could even imagine she felt the feather-soft touch of his mustache gliding against her cheek. It was a lovely dream.

In the morning she was highly flustered when she woke up and found herself in his arms.

"Hello, sleepyhead," Richard said when she stirred.

"Good morning." Her voice quivered as she spoke.

He brought his arms over his head and stretched. "Would you like to go out for breakfast?" he asked.

Sarah shook her head. "No thanks. What I'd like is a good hot shower."

"I don't suppose you need my help?" Richard teased.

Sarah closed her eyes and groaned.

"I guess that means I should leave now."

She walked him to the door. "Thanks again for staying."

He kissed the tip of her nose. "Anytime. That's what friends are for." With that, he left.

Friends? Is that what he considered her? A friend? Her mind was too muddled to make sense out of anything at the moment. She'd never thought of herself as being dependent on anyone. Apparently she was. On Richard Collier, a man with plans for the future that didn't include her.

Richard called her that afternoon to check on her and to invite her to go to the circus with him the following Saturday. Sarah declined. She assured him that she would continue to look for the right house for him. Maintaining a business relationship seemed the best position to take.

Her mother phoned the next day, the moment she arrived back home, and asked if she could come over that evening for the dinner they'd planned before she went to Paris. She said there was something important she needed to discuss with Sarah.

Sarah didn't have a clue as to what kind of predicament her mother had gotten herself into this time, but judging from some of her past fiascoes, she knew to expect the unexpected.

Andora arrived an hour late, which Sarah knew was typical. She greeted her mother at the door and took several white bags from her gloved hands.

"Sarah! I've missed you," Andora said, giving her

a hug. "Did anything exciting happen while I was gone?"

Sarah told her about the robbery, and that was all. She knew what kind of reaction she would get if she mentioned Richard's name.

"Let's sit at your coffee table and eat Oriental-style," Andora suggested. Sarah went to the kitchen to fetch plates and silverware. Her mother followed and made a pot of tea.

When they were seated on the floor, Andora quite casually asked, "Dear, do you remember George Miller?"

Sarah had to think for a minute. "The man who lives two doors from you and grows the lovely roses. Didn't he plant tulip bulbs for you last fall?"

Andora nodded and spooned fried rice onto her plate. "George has a huge greenhouse and grows hybrid orchids too. And, he's always been a good neighbor, but that's not why I mentioned him."

Curious, Sarah stared at her mother intently. Did Mr. Miller have his sights set on her mother's banking accounts to support his horticulture interests? Her former stepfathers hadn't hesitated to dip into her mother's savings.

Andora reached for a cup from the tray and gestured toward the pot. "Why don't you serve some tea, dear, then we can discuss my dilemma."

Sarah's fingers froze on the handle. "Are you in

some kind of trouble?'' She attempted to pour without scalding herself.

Andora laughed, but unsteadily. ''That depends on what you'd define as trouble.'' Again she laughed and took a serving of chow mein. She sighed and looked at Sarah.

''Mother, what is it?'' Sarah studied her with growing concern. This was definitely not the Andora Lavelle she knew, the lively, entertaining woman who radiated confidence. Her mother was downright jittery. ''Has George Miller done something to you?'' Sarah prompted.

Andora took a sip of tea, then another. She swallowed and emitted a long sigh. ''He did something very unexpected,'' she began, speaking very slowly.

''And? Go on.''

''Remember when I invited you to join me in Europe?''

''Yes, and I couldn't get away for that much time.''

Andora nodded. ''I'd already purchased a ticket for you. I gave it to George.''

''Why on earth did you do that?'' Sarah wanted to know.

''His wife passed away a few years ago, and he seemed so lonely. Sarah, I'm lonely, too. George and I have been going out to the theater every now and then, and he's been over to my house for dinner.''

Sarah nodded her understanding. She knew all about loneliness.

"So, we spent time together in Paris. He'd served in France during the war and hadn't been back since. We visited places he'd seen and went to quiet villages and went dancing. He's such a good dancer . . . ." Her voice suddenly trailed off.

"Mother?"

"He asked me to marry him."

Sarah closed her eyes and leaned back against the sofa.

"I suppose you think I'm a foolish old woman."

"It's your decision, Mother," Sarah said non-comittally.

"You're right. It is. And speaking of decisions, what have you decided to do about Richard Collier?"

Sarah climbed onto the sofa. "Why are you asking about him?"

Andora smiled. "When I called you this morning, I spoke with Evelyn a few minutes first, and she told me about the panda."

"Great! The entire situation has been blown out of proportion. When will the gossip stop?"

"Have you been seeing him?" her mother asked.

"He's a client."

"Pshaw! Be honest with yourself, Sarah. Do you look forward to being with him? Does your heart go all fluttery when you answer the phone and it's him? Do you find yourself thinking of things you want to tell him?"

Sarah gnawed her bottom lip.

"Well?" Andora prompted.

"Yes," Sarah whispered, hating herself for taking the bait.

"Finally!" Andora exclaimed. "Those are the same feelings I have for George. I can tell you from first hand experience, my dear daughter. You've fallen in love."

A hot tear slid down Sarah's cheek, and she sniffed back a sob. "I don't want to be in love."

Andora joined her daughter on the sofa and wrapped an arm around Sarah's shoulders. "Why? This should be the happiest time of your life. I just don't understand why you're so distraught . . . unless . . . Does Richard love you?"

Sarah shook her head. "He only considers me a friend. I think he probably has a relationship with someone else. He's awfully anxious to buy a house."

"He hasn't mentioned being engaged, has he?"

"No."

Andora slapped her hand down on top of the coffee table with a resounding smack. "Then why in the world aren't you going after him? He's fair game until the ring's on his hand."

Again, Sarah shook her head. "I can't."

"That doesn't make any sense. Of course you can. What's stopping you?"

Sarah sniffled back her tears and shrugged.

Andora hefted her purse from the floor and pulled out a tissue for Sarah. "It's past time that we've had a little talk. I've got to ask you a question, and I want you to be absolutely honest with me.''

''Okay.''

''Have I made you afraid to love?''

Sarah lifted her tear-stained face to her mother's and tried to swallow around the huge lump that blocked her throat. A single choked word was her only response. ''Yes.''

Andora released a heavy breath. ''I haven't set a very good example for you, have I, Sarah?''

''Marriage hasn't always brought you happiness,'' Sarah said simply.

''No, it certainly hasn't,'' her mother readily agreed. ''But each time I married, it was a different set of circumstances. I didn't always marry for love.''

''You didn't?'' Sarah gasped.

''Of course not. After your father died, I couldn't even define love. I married because of loneliness, boredom, middle-age-crises.'' She paused momentarily to catch her breath. ''My reasoning seemed sound at the time, but every time I landed in divorce court, I realized I'd tied myself to a man for all the wrong reasons.''

''What about this time?'' Sarah had to know.

A bright smile lit Andora's face. ''This time it's the real thing. I love George Miller with all my heart, and he's crazy about me.''

''Are you afraid you'll lose him?''

''I'm not dwelling on the fact that George and I aren't youngsters anymore.'' Andora squeezed Sarah's hand. "Whether we have thirty years together or thirty days, it will be just that. Time spent together. I'll be satisfied with the present and let the future take care of itself."

Sarah smiled and gave her mother a tight hug. "I'm so happy for you, Mother. When's the wedding?"

"Saturday," Andora told her. "We want to get married right away."

"How will you manage to plan a wedding in such a short amount of time?" Sarah exclaimed.

Andora patted her hand. "George and I want a simple ceremony. Tonight he's calling his son from Cleveland to ask if he'll stand up with him, and I was hoping you'd do the same for me."

"I'd be honored," Sarah said. "Would you like me to invite your friends over here for a reception afterward?"

"That's a lovely offer, dear, but we're planning to marry early in the day and fly to Las Vegas that afternoon for our honeymoon. And, Sarah, if you'd like to invite Richard, it's okay with me."

Sarah gave a weak smile. Inviting Richard was the last thing she would do.

Chapter 12

Evelyn was quizzing Sarah about the details of her mother's wedding the following Saturday afternoon when the front door of Middletown Realty swung open. Evelyn groaned. Sarah knew without even turning around who had just walked in. The overpowering scent of perfume wafted through the air. She glanced over her shoulder to see a stunning redhead wearing a full-length black mink coat waltz through the reception area.

"Hello, everybody! I'm home!" the woman exclaimed, punctuating her greeting with an exaggerated giggle, the trademark of only one person—Charlotte Knox.

Charlotte sashayed down the hall, announcing to all within earshot that she had "big news." When she returned to the lobby, several fellow agents followed on her heels. Swinging her briefcase in her typical flirtatious fashion, she said, "You all won't believe what I have tucked inside here." She patted the leather satchel and giggled again. "Go ahead. Guess," she challenged the others.

"A contract signed by the president to sell the White House," one man ventured, causing an uproar of laughter.

"Almost as good," Charlotte cooed. She carelessly tossed her coat over a chair before continuing. "I just listed a honey of a house in Brookway Heights. A century-old Tudor, move-in condition. The owner is a grumpy old goat of a man who wants to move to Florida with his son. He wants out fast and he's ready to sell. He also wants to get rid of some of his old furniture."

Sarah's brows rose. The house was in the area Richard would like to move to. And a Tudor? She stepped closer to Charlotte and patiently waited for the barrage of questions on room size and exact location to cease before saying, "I'd like to take a look at the house right away."

Charlotte brought her hand to her mouth. "Well, I declare, Sarah, you sure are hot to trot on this one."

Silently Sarah fumed. Charlotte's atrocious attempt at a southern accent was nauseating. Sarah knew the woman had been born and bred in Chicago and used the dialect to . . . well, to lure innocent people into her clutches.

Sarah swallowed her anger. As much as the idea repulsed her, she needed to ask Charlotte a favor. "I've been working with a client who's expressed an interest in an older Tudor." Sarah swallowed again. "Could you wait until, say tomorrow morning, before putting it in the computer?"

"Not list it right away!" Charlotte exclaimed loud enough to be heard out on the street. "Are you sure you have a buyer on the hook?"

Even her cutesy phrases got under Sarah's skin. Yet, she didn't want to appear annoyed. "My client is bona fide. I'd like to show him the house tonight."

"Him?" Charlotte gasped. "Don't tell me there's a man qualified to buy in Brookway Heights who escaped my attention. Is he that dentist you've been working with?"

Sarah gave a saccharin smile. "He's the one," was all the information she provided.

Charlotte shrugged. "I can't win them all, I guess." She giggled again. "Oh well, I promise not to leak the facts until tomorrow. But after I do, just stand back. That house probably won't stay on the market a week. And the commission will mean another cruise for me! Oh, happy day."

Happy day, indeed, Sarah thought, instantly suspicious of the asking price. "Could I talk with you for a minute in my office, Charlotte? And, please bring a copy of the contract with you."

"I have to make a phone call, then I'll be there," Charlotte called over her shoulder.

Returning to her office, Sarah turned on her computer and keyed in the code to provide a printout of the last quarter selling prices for the homes in Brookway Heights. She was scanning the figures when Charlotte appeared.

"I've been meaning to come and see you," she said without a trace of her accent.

"Oh?" Sarah gestured for Charlotte to sit. "What did you want to see me about?"

"It's the contract issue. When will I earn the right to do my own work?"

"I thought Bradley and I made it clear when we hired you that for sixty days—"

"That's completely absurd! It's also unproductive," Charlotte complained. "Either you or Bradley have henpecked my contracts to death. I've been in the business long enough to know how to list a house."

Sarah refused to be baited. She simply extended her arm for the papers. Charlotte reluctantly handed them over. Everything on the first two pages was standard information and looked correct. However, when she turned to the last sheet, Sarah nearly went into orbit.

"This listing price is way out of line! It's at least thirty percent higher than any other home on the market in Brookway Heights." She pointed to the figures on the printout.

"I know, I know. But this house has more square feet than most of them," Charlotte justified.

"Not according to the selling records," Sarah countered.

"Wait just a minute," Charlotte said, wagging a finger at Sarah. "You want me to adjust the price so your buyer can qualify. Nothing doing." She defiantly crossed her arms across her chest.

"That isn't the way I do business," Sarah returned, mustering every ounce of patience she possessed. "I don't believe in appealing to greed. I prefer to set a realistic price on properties and not to encourage my clients to put outrageous prices on their homes."

Charlotte gave a complacent laugh which grated on Sarah's ears. "With all the corporate transfers, we're bound to get a good price on that old house. I've worked with a lot of executives, and they're loaded! They don't think twice about spending tons of money."

"The increase in prices of upscale homes might be good news to you, Charlotte, but you seem to forget that the minute prices go up, it means that young couples down at the bottom of the salary scale are priced out of the market. And, older folks who want a condo or a smaller house are forced to move away from an area where they might have lived all their lives."

"I never thought of it that way," Charlotte admitted. "So what should I do now?"

"I suggest you phone your client and explain your error."

Charlotte expelled a pent-up breath and stood. "Okay. I'll rework the figures and call the old man, er, my client, to see if he'll agree to the new terms. If he does, do you still want to show the place?" she asked, all coyness gone from her sudden brisk tone.

"Definitely," Sarah told her. "As soon as possible."

When Charlotte had gone Sarah stared blindly at the

computer screen. If the house was anything like the glowing description she'd received, Richard would probably fall in love with the place. Then he wouldn't have any other reason to continue seeing her. She'd never been less anxious to show a house in her life.

She turned off the computer and dialed Richard's number. After five rings, his answering machine came on. Sarah sighed and decided to phone his office.

"Doctors Collier and Williams. How may I help you?" a cheerful voice asked.

"Is Doctor Collier available?" Sarah queried.

"He's with a patient," the woman returned. "Are you calling to schedule an appointment?"

"This is Sarah Perkins calling and—"

"Oh, yes," his receptionist interrupted. "Dr. Collier said anytime you called I should get him right away. Hold the line please."

A few minutes later Richard's deep voice resounded in her ear. "Sarah, what a surprise. Did you decide you could break away long enough to go to the circus after all?"

"No, actually I'm calling because I may have found a house for you. It's a Tudor in Brookway Heights."

"Wonderful. Have you seen it?"

"No, it was just listed this morning, and I was hoping we could go over together shortly."

"Sorry, but I can't today. I have an emergency crown repair scheduled for three o'clock. How about sometime tomorrow?"

"That may be a problem," Sarah said, trying to keep the disappointment from her voice. "The listing agent has agreed to give me an exclusive showing. We really should take a look today."

"This could be the real thing?"

"Quite possibly. Would you be able to meet me at the office early this evening?"

"I thought you had other plans."

"I can cancel them."

"But not to go to the circus?"

"Richard—"

"Okay, okay. I get the message. Richard the client takes precedent over Richard the companion."

"I'm sorry, but—"

"There's no need to explain, Sarah. I understand perfectly." He cleared his throat. "My office is close to the Brookway Heights area. Why don't you meet me at the house at five-thirty?"

"I'll be there," Sarah replied, then gave him the address. After they said their good-byes and she replaced the receiver, she emitted a long sigh. He'd made her appear so . . . so callous. How utterly absurd that he could make her feel that way when she worked so hard to find him the perfect home.

And furthermore, she didn't need to justify how she spent every minute. What she did on her own time was her business. Surely he hadn't expected that she would be available to flit her time away every Saturday, or had he? She needed time to spend with other clients.

But was it right to devote every spare second to them, a little voice questioned?

Sarah took a deep breath of pine-scented air as she stepped from her Bronco. It was almost twilight, and the setting sun streaked the clouds with soft hues of lavender, pink, and blue, providing a magnificent background for the stately Tudor. It sat naturally atop a terraced lawn that rolled gently down on the south side to a lake. Massive white pine trees blocked the view of neighboring homes, creating a secluded atmosphere.

At the sound of a car, Sarah turned to see Richard pulling in behind her. She warned herself sternly not to reveal the effect he had on her. Especially not now. However, composing herself was not easy. She barely had time to pull herself together before he opened his door. She managed to smile as he walked toward her.

He was smiling too. Their eyes met and held in the sudden silence as they looked at one another. It was Sarah who finally spoke, almost stammering as her heart pounded uncontrollably. "Shall we go inside?"

"I'd go with you anywhere," he replied with a grin.

Sarah drew a ragged breath and preceded him up the walk.

The moment she opened the front door, Sarah instinctively knew Richard had found his home. He followed her inside. She immediately assumed a professional air and led him from room to room. He was quiet, attentive. Each time she turned to him, she found his gaze upon her. She wasn't certain he had even paid attention to what she'd been discussing. His strange behavior was disconcerting to say the least.

Her knees were shaking as she climbed the steps to the second floor. Richard looked around, still making no comments. Sarah stood in the wide upstairs hallway and watched him walk in and out of each room. She noted that his pace was slow. Were his eyes narrowing critically? She wondered as he ventured into the smallest of the five bedrooms. She followed him inside.

''I know the hardwood floor needs refinishing, and of course, the wallpaper needs to be replaced,'' she said.

''The ceiling should be repainted,'' Richard added, obviously guessing that since Sarah was looking up her next comment was bound to be about the ceiling. ''Yes, I'm aware that the room needs work. I'm not opposed to spending some time and money refinishing it.'' Then he walked over to a closet and opened the door. ''Plenty of space in here.''

''The house does have ample storage,'' Sarah agreed.

''I think this room would make a perfect nursery, don't you think so?''

Sarah nodded miserably as she stared at the empty room. Someday Richard's babies would sleep in here. She could almost envision a whimsical pastel wallpaper accenting the now faded walls . . . a rocking chair in the corner . . . a crib at the far end of the room . . . a toy chest with a gigantic panda bear sitting on the top. Her bear, but not her baby.

The realization that Richard and his wife would stand together, arm in arm and peer into the crib and watch their precious little one sleep, tore at Sarah's heart. Her shoulders drooped. Without looking at him, she spoke in a small throaty voice. "I'll meet you downstairs." She turned to go.

"Wait a minute, Sarah." He reached for her hand. "Don't you want to take another look around up here?"

"No," she said in a somber tone, attempting to withdraw her hand from his.

"Perhaps this isn't the right house then," he stated flatly.

Sarah's eyes flickered up to his, momentarily in confusion. "If you feel right about it, there's no reason not to buy it," she said, her spirits sinking even further. "I thought you were ready to write a contract."

"Are you?"

Sarah sighed deeply. "It's a lovely home. I honestly think you'd be happy here."

He held her gaze for earth-stopping moments. "Would you like to go out for dinner and talk about it?"

"No," she whispered.

Richard released her hand and raked his fingers through his hair. "Before we leave, could you give me the dimensions of each of the bedrooms again? I don't want to forget."

As they walked back down the hall, Sarah stood outside the rooms, reading from the information sheet.

When they came to the master bedroom, Richard gestured for Sarah to precede him inside. "This room has a balcony that overlooks the terraced backyard," she read. "It features a large bathroom with his-and-her sinks and two walk-in closets."

Richard remained silent and stared at her. Sarah folded the spec sheet and tucked it into the pocket of her coat. "Have you seen enough?" she asked with much more agitation than she'd intended.

Richard gave her an odd look. "Would you like to go down to the kitchen table and hammer out a contract?"

Sarah sighed. Usually this was the best part of being a realtor. She had successfully matched a buyer to a home. She should feel elated. Instead, she felt miserable.

She trudged back down the steps and spoke over her shoulder to Richard. "Since it's so late, if you don't mind, I'd rather work on the contract tomorrow. In my office," she added as an afterthought.

"That's fine by me. Shouldn't we at least go out for a drink to celebrate?"

Sarah turned to face him at the bottom of the stairs. "That may be a little premature. Your offer hasn't been accepted yet."

"When it is, then will you let me take you to dinner?"

Sarah tried to swallow around a burning sensation in the back of her throat. "Yes." she murmured, her eyes downcast.

"And tonight, shouldn't we even shake hands?"

Acknowledging his gesture, Sarah valiantly extended a slightly unsteady hand toward him. Richard enclosed her trembling fingers within the hard strength of his own, but then did not release them. Instead his glance settled on her crestfallen features. "You're shaking," he observed. "Are you cold?"

"No," she disclaimed.

"Then what? I don't understand. I thought this house was something special, and now you're obviously upset and anxious to get out of here. Didn't you tell me that was a sign of not being interested?"

Sarah drew a painful breath, not wanting to explain, but knowing she must. "You've found a lovely home—"

"We found it together, Sarah," he corrected.

"Okay, we found it together."

"So tell me, is this a house you could live in?"

Sarah rubbed the bridge of her nose. "Richard, I show dozens of houses every month, but I don't plan on living in any of them. I honestly try not to influence my clients one way or the other. I'm a professional—"

"Will you stop with the Madame Realtor routine? I want your opinion, Sarah. Could you be comfortable living in this house?"

Oh, he wanted to know too much, far more than she

could easily explain. Why couldn't he just leave well enough alone? Sarah closed her eyes. She wanted him to be happy, to buy the house. But the thought of him living in it with another woman tore her heart in two.

She forced herself to meet his eyes. "I could live here forever," she said honestly.

For several long, heart-wrenching seconds Richard said nothing. He merely stood there staring at her. Finally, he took a step closer to her and cleared his throat. "Then you agree that this would be a place where two people could share their lives with each other?"

"Yes," Sarah answered in a choked whisper. She shut her eyes against a gathering sense of foreboding, then felt Richard's fingers cup her face.

"Look at me, Sarah," he commanded softly.

When she did, her breath caught on a sob.

Richard exhaled heavily, brushed her hair back from her face then supported his hands on her shoulders. "You know, for being such an intelligent, perceptive woman, sometimes you can be a little dense."

"What! You've tortured me with all your prodding and now you're insulting me!" she blurted in a rush. Her nervous indignation had her in its grip. "I'm leaving."

"Oh, Sarah," he breathed. His arms went around her and drew her into a tight embrace. "I've been hoping beyond hope that I could convince you we'd be perfect for each other." His voice grew husky with emotion, and he took in a long, ragged breath before he continued. "This home is for you, Sarah."

She drew back to gaze at him in wonder. "For me?" she gasped, certain she'd misunderstood.

"I was hoping you'd let me share it with you," Richard added, then smiled.

"Share it with you?" she repeated, still dumbfounded.

"Sit down," he said, "here on the steps." When she had, he faced her on bended knee and took her hands in his. "For the rest of my life, I want to share all that I have with you. I love you, Sarah."

A mixture of relief and exhilaration flooded her. "Oh, Richard, I love you too," she said, gathering him into her arms. "It feels so good to finally say the words. I've kept them inside for so long."

He gently pulled away from her and grinned. Sarah's heart turned over in her chest. "I suspected some time ago that you may have not been as indifferent as you wanted to be, or were determined to be."

"Yes, well, right from the beginning you made me feel so confused I didn't know what was happening to me," she confessed shyly. "Then when I realized how I felt, there wasn't anything I could do."

Richard gazed at her incredulously. "Are you telling me you knew you were in love with me when we were in St. Maarten?"

Sarah nodded shakily.

"Why didn't you say something?"

"I didn't know what to say."

"So I wound up buying a house just so I could see you again."

Sarah's eyes opened wider. "I thought you wanted to buy a house!" she exclaimed.

"I wanted you," Richard clarified. "A month ago, buying a house was the last thing I'd ever expected to become involved with. But after I came back from the Caribbean, I found myself becoming rather intrigued with the idea."

"Why?" Sarah asked.

Richard kissed the tip of her nose. "Because I found myself confronted with one very beautiful, but very stubborn, independent woman who became necessary for my happiness. A fabulous home is an added bonus." With that, he rose to his feet and pulled Sarah into his arms.

She looked into his eyes and saw the love she had never dared to dream he would feel for her reflected there. Slowly Richard lowered his head, his lips tenderly claiming hers.

What more wonderful way could she live the rest of her life than by spending it with Richard? With the man she loved, Sarah had found the home of her dreams, her own paradise on earth.